POWDER CHARGE

Morgan stood the gunman up and slammed a quick left and then a right fist into his face before the surprised man could defend himself. He jolted backwards against the hotel wall where Morgan caught him and powered two fists into the man's belly.

Lee rammed his right knee upward, caught the man's chin and snapped his head back, dumping him into the alley half unconscious. It took a half-dozen slaps across his face to bring the man back to the talking stage.

"Why did you swing that bomb into my room?" Morgan demanded, holding one hand loosely around the man's throat. He gurgled and Morgan eased the pressure.

"Damn, not my idea. Some gent paid me."

"Who, damn you! Who paid you to kill me?"

BUCKSKIN #25

POWDER CHARGE

KIT DALTON

LEISURE BOOKS   NEW YORK CITY

A LEISURE BOOK®

April 2005

Published by

Dorchester Publishing Co., Inc.
200 Madison Avenue
New York, NY 10016

ISBN 0-8439-2754-2

The name "Leisure Books" and the stylized "L" with design are trademarks of Dorchester Publishing Co., Inc.

Printed in the United States of America.

Visit us on the web at www.dorchesterpub.com.

POWDER CHARGE

Chapter One

He rode into the little town of La Grande feeling worn out, hot, dirty, tired of forking a horse and all around killing mean. If anybody crossed him today, Lee Morgan swore they would be dead before they even knew he had reached for his iron.

Morgan looked as bad as he felt. He had a two week growth of beard, shaggy hair, wore the same clothes he had put on a month ago, and not a bath for three weeks. He'd been on the Owl Hoot Trail for two months, dodging a posse and two bounty hunters. All of them were after the wrong man, but he wasn't about to stop and tell them how wrong they were. Words never did beat bullets, and Lee knew sure as hell that dead men didn't tell tales.

This wasn't a town, it was a rat's nest: two blocks of main street, rows of whorehouses and saloons, one church, and ten stores that probably didn't have what you needed anyway.

He slid off the roan.

"Whiskey and food for me," he rasped to the tired animal, "then if you're lucky, some hay and maybe some oats for you in the livery. If there is a livery."

Morgan wrapped the reins around the rail and walked with a slight limp as he rolled up to the boardwalk with a cowboy's gait. Dead ahead was the Gunsmoke Saloon. Probably aptly named.

Two months is two months too long to be on the run. He was through running. If the damn bounty hunters followed him this far, either they would die or he would. Right now it didn't make one hell of a lot of difference to Morgan which way it went.

He pushed through the bat wings and gave his pupils time to adjust so he could see the place. It had a wooden floor, a real bar and half a dozen card tables. No whores pretending to be dance hall girls. Christ he hated that. A slut was a slut, why did she have to sugar coat her profession?

He moved to the bar. Half the men in the place watched him, not just a casual glance, but a steady stare, damn near a challenge. He glared right back at them, threw down a quarter eagle gold piece on the bar, and asked for a bottle of whiskey and a glass.

The bar was polished hardwood, stained and varnished and waxed until it shone. A lot of damn hard work on that wood. The apron brought back the bottle and a dollar greenback and a silver fifty cent piece. Morgan looked at the greenback a long time, then up at the barkeep who tried to stare him down.

"Greenbacks good as gold around here,

stranger," the apron said and wiped the bar as he moved on down the line.

Morgan pocketed it and grabbed the bottle and glass. He slumped into a chair at the closest table where he could sit with his back to the wall and a view of the entrance. He popped the cork from the bottle, splashed the glass half full, and took a long pull.

The cough came on cue, short and harsh. He grimaced, looked at the cheap whiskey and threw down the rest of it that remained in the glass. This time there was no cough.

A tall, thin man walked up to the table. He held a deck of cards in his hand and pretended to drop them, then caught them neatly.

"Oh, sorry. Want to start a new game of poker? The other one is pretty well filled."

"Can't afford it," Morgan said.

The gambler's hands reverted to form and neatly cut the cards with one hand. He grinned. "Didn't expect you to play. This ain't my kind of game. Man wants to see you in the back room. He owns this place and about half the town. His name is Rudolph P. Merriweather. You're not supposed to recognize the name."

"Why would I want to talk to him?"

"May I sit down?"

Morgan shrugged and poured another shot of whiskey. He didn't offer any to the stranger.

The gambler sat down. He spread out the cards in a fan and laid them on the table. In the middle of the pasteboards Morgan saw a twenty dollar bill.

"Mr. Merriweather says he wants to hire you. He has a job for you but you can turn him down. This twenty dollar bill is just to get you interested in considering talking to him."

Morgan hadn't seen a twenty dollar bill since he left California two months ago. The grub line trail had been his cafe and the hard ground under the stars his hotel. He looked at the twenty dollar bill. He wanted it.

"Go ahead, take it. Looks like you're on the far end of a long stick."

Morgan looked up frowning.

"No offense. Just a southern expression that means it's hard times and it's been the hardest of all for you. Mr. Merriweather will bring in a good steak dinner for you from the hotel with all the fixings and some fine cold beer to go with it. All he asks is that you go to his office and talk to him. You can even keep your gun."

Morgan shifted in his chair but his gaze never left the end of the greenback on the poker table. "I never do straight killings."

The gambler picked up the cards and the paper bill fluttered toward Morgan who grabbed it before it blew off the table.

"I don't know what Mr. Merriweather has in mind, but he doesn't go around hiring someone to murder people. I can assure you of that. He's a respected businessman here in La Grande. I've known him for ten years. He owns this saloon. He's waiting, if you would care to come now. You can bring the bottle with you."

The greenback single in his pocket was the last dollar that Morgan owned. Maybe it was about time he took some gainful employment. He stared at the gambler.

"Why did he pick me for the job?"

"That one I can answer," the gambler said. "Your gun is tied down, your hands are quick and you have the eyes and move like a gunman."

Morgan tossed down the next shot of whiskey. It wasn't the worst booze he'd ever tasted, but damn close. He put his hand on the bottle and looked at the gambler.

The man's face was white and soft, close shaven and smelled of talc and some kind of bay rum. The gambler took out a gold watch from his vest pocket, flipped open the cover and looked at the time.

"If we leave the table in another 30 seconds, you earn two more of those twenty dollar bills."

Morgan grabbed the bottle and stood. "Which way?" he asked.

The gambler handed him two more new, crisp and clean twenty dollar greenbacks.

"Right this way, sir," the gambler said, a knowing smile on his thin face. He'd be good at poker facing anyone.

They went to the end of the bar and behind it to a door built into the wall so it didn't look like a door. It swung inward and there was no knob. Past the door Morgan saw they were in a storage area for boxes of whiskey, beer and glasses.

The gambler pointed to a door. "Oh, my name is Ormley if you ever need an honest game of poker. I play here at the Gunsmoke." He opened the door, stepped aside and let Morgan enter.

The room was set up like a fancy parlor. It had a woman's touch. The floor held a thick carpet, pictures tastefully decorated the walls, a window looked out on the alley that had no houses beyond it so the view carried west to snow frosted mountains.

Furniture was both living room and office, he noticed, including a large business desk of heavy walnut, cabinets and twin lamps on swivels mounted on the front of the desk. A small man with thin gray hair, wrinkled skin and deep set, brilliant blue eyes sat behind the clean top of the desk. He wore a green eye shade in the fashion of an accountant, and looked up after marking his place on a document with his finger.

"Ah, yes, the gunman. Older than I expected." He sighed. Morgan guessed he was nearly 80, maybe more. He moved slowly as he turned from the desk in a swivel chair. An old hand with more bones than flesh pointed to a chair.

"Sit, I don't like craning my neck up to look at you." He stared for a moment as Morgan sat on the soft, upholstered chair. He hadn't touched one in six months.

"You look a mite worn out to be coming looking for work," the old man said. "Oh, my manners. I'm Merriweather, the man who wrote you the letter."

Morgan stood.

"What'n hell?"

Morgan walked to the door and the old face turned and watched.

"What'n hell you doing, whippersnapper?"

Morgan chuckled. "Ain't been called that in a coon's age. Mr. Merriweather, I'm just passing through. I didn't get a letter from you. I'm the wrong man."

Merriweather motioned with his hand. "You take money from me?"

Morgan nodded.

"Then sit your ass down in my chair until I get my money's worth."

Morgan chuckled again. He hadn't laughed in a month. He did owe the man a few more minutes for his sixty dollars. He went back to the chair and sat.

"But you are a gunman. Can tell the way you move, way your eyes take in a whole room and everyone in it in one quick glance, then you concentrate on what could be any trouble. Seen it before. You are a gunhand?"

"Not as such, but I can get a hog leg out of leather better'n a few now in their graves."

Merriweather cackled a high satisfying laugh. "Knew so. Now we're getting somewhere. Simple little job. One round should do it, if'n you're as good as your looks indicate." The old man watched him. "Want that dinner and some cold beer? Whiskey ain't much with a steak."

Lee nodded and at once the door opened and the gambler Ormley came in with a fancy little rolling cart that had a complete steak dinner on it, silverware, a linen napkin and three bottles of beer so cold they were sweating.

The gambler looked at Merriweather who flicked his hand and Ormley retreated.

Morgan hadn't seen a steak or a spread like this in three months. It had been a hard summer. He shook out the napkin, put it over his filthy pants legs and eased up to the rolling dinner table. His first bite was out of the steak, done on the outside, red, juicy and just a touch of blood left inside.

Merriweather laughed softly. "I see you're a man who likes a good steak. Fine. I never trust a man who won't eat a steak."

He settled in his big chair. "Young man, you go right ahead and enjoy your dinner. I'll catch a quick nap. I don't sleep much good at night, so I enjoy naps now and then. Hell, I'm eighty-five

and I can do damned near anything I want to."
He snorted. "Damn near, and that's the biggest
reason that I need to talk to you. Take your time,
enjoy your steak dinner."

The old man let the back of the chair recline
until he was almost lying down, then closed his
eyes. He was sleeping in twenty seconds.

Morgan chewed the steak, shook his head at
the folly of the man. Going to sleep in his office
with a stranger there? Morgan shrugged and
went back to the meal. Best food he'd eaten in . . .
damn, how long? Maybe it was time he settled
down for a little gainful employment. He just
hoped to hell that the last bounty hunter had lost
his trail.

When the last of the mashed potatoes and
gravy was gone and the final bite of steak
savored and swallowed, Merriweather swung up
in the chair and swiveled it around to face
Morgan. He stared at Morgan for a moment.
When Morgan dropped his used napkin on the
tray, the door he had entered by opened and
Ormley came in and left just as quickly with the
remains of the meal on the rolling dinner cart.

When the door closed, Merriweather lifted a
sheaf of bills. He riffled through them and
Morgan saw a series of the number 20 time after
time.

"If you do the job I have for you, I'll give you
this stack of twenty-dollar bills. To satisfy your
curiosity, there are fifty of them here—that's a
thousand U.S. dollars. More money than the
average store clerk makes in three years. A
thousand dollars is one hell of a lot of cash."

Merriweather paused a moment. "Not sure
you can do the job I need done. I figured that the

Abilene Kid could do it. He shoots down people all the time. I sent him a letter and some money. But you're not the Abilene Kid."

"Damn well better not be," Morgan said. "He got himself hung last month down in Arizona. Shot up a town, killed the sheriff, got wounded and captured, and three days later they hung the little bastard."

"Life can be trying sometimes. My name is Rudolph P. Merriweather. Just what's your name, young man?"

"Lee Morgan, sometimes of Boise, Idaho, but usually from points west and southwest."

The old man held out his hand. Morgan got up and shook it and felt as if he'd just caught hold of a skeleton. He sat down again

"Are you a wanted man, Mr. Morgan?"

"Have been times. Gross miscarriage of justice. Self defense every time."

"But you have killed people, mostly men I would guess, and it didn't ruin your life."

"I guess you could say that."

"Good, because I want you to kill someone for me."

"I don't do flat out murder for nobody, Mr. Merriweather. I'll give you back your money and be on my way." He stood and fished the three bills from his pocket.

The derringer came in the old man's hand out of nowhere and Morgan felt the prickle of a challenge on the back of his neck.

"Sit down, young man. Not even you can outdraw a weapon aimed at your wide gut. Sit down!" The last came sharply and Morgan looked at the frail old man and suddenly saw the humor in it. He sat and grinned.

"Both bark and a bite, right, Merriweather?"

"Everywhere but in my pecker. Don't jump to conclusions, I don't want you to murder, just hurry along the natural death process a little."

"Could you explain that, Mr. Merriweather? I'm not sure I know what the difference is."

"It's simple. I'll pay you a thousand dollars to kill—me."

Chapter Two

Morgan looked up quickly.

"What the hell did you say, old man?"

"I said you get your thousand dollars just as soon as you kill me. Everything is ready. Fact is, I've been waiting for the Kid for two months."

"Why not just jump off a high rimrock?"

"Might hurt a lot and I might not die. Besides, I have an image here in La Grande to protect."

"Good one or a bad one?"

Merriweather leaned back and laughed. At the same time he put the small pistol away in his vest pocket.

"Choice, yes, choice. I'm afraid it's a rather positive image, and my granddaughter would be upset as well. I want to be remembered, well thought of, leave my mark on the community."

"This is sounding crazier all the time."

"I have a feeling that you're not going to whip out your .45, blast me through the heart and take the offered one thousand dollars?"

"Damn right, I'm not! Last time I bought in cheap on a sure thing it turned out to be a whole bucketful of snakes, and I'm not rid of the bastards yet. I don't do anything unless I know everything about it, what happens next, and who is involved."

"Easy," the old man said. "I own about half the town. Came here in Sixty One and put down the streets and platted it out. Then I brought in settlers and ranchers. Put advertisements in the Portland papers. I left the whole south side of the street for someone else to homestead or buy.

"A man did. We don't get on. He put up the hotel and the stores and some houses. His tastes run to wood, as in lumber, as in logging and saw-milling.

"I'm a meat and potatoes man myself, mostly beef. Does that spell it out enough?"

"You haven't even got started. You own one side of town, he owns the other. How did trees and beef get into it?"

"Don't need to know. Matter of fact, I won't tell you. Offer still stands. I'll tell Ormley. The cash will be in his keeping. Anytime I turn up dead, you get the thousand. Now, it's time for my afternoon nap. Close the door softly, young man, as you leave."

Merriweather leaned back in the chair and closed his eyes.

Morgan stood gently but still the chair squeaked. The old man opened one eye. "Feel free right now to blast me, if you want to—unless you need to establish an alibi. Yes, I see. All right. Sooner the better far as I'm concerned."

"I told you—"

"Don't want to hear it. At my age I get most anything I want, get to do most anything I can. So don't disappoint me." He closed his eye and left both shut as Morgan walked to the door and went out. He slammed it.

Inside the office he heard Rudolph P. Merriweather cackle out his raucous laugh.

Morgan stepped through the door and found Ormley waiting for him.

"So?" he asked.

"So what?" Morgan countered.

"Mr. Merriweather said I was to function as your aide, to fetch and carry, to summon and be summoned. Are you working for him or not?"

"Depends. I need a lot more information. Is there a good cup of coffee in this excuse for a town?"

They talked for half an hour at a small coffee shop which served home made pie and doughnuts as well. When the chawing was over, Morgan had a much better picture of the small town of La Grande, Oregon, of Merriweather, and a gent named Slocom Wert.

Wert was the second man in town and owned the other half. He also owned a large tract of land in the Wallowa Mountains which began about twenty miles due west of town. He was a sawmill man, but there was no cheap way to get the sawed lumber out of the mountains and to the Columbia River, 80 miles to the northwest.

Then the key words came. *Raidroad line.* It was due to push east and south through the corner of Oregon down to the middle of Idaho and on to Boise.

"And Wert wants to route the rails through the

edge of the mountains to pick up his lumber,"
Morgan said.

"True, but Mr. Merriweather wants them to
come the shorter route through La Grande and
service the town and the cattle owners who bring
their herds in here for driving them to the
Columbia River. The railroad will help everyone,
but just where it goes will make or break a
fortune."

"That road is two or three years away,"
Morgan said. "Merriweather might not live that
long."

"That, Mr. Morgan, is why he wants it set up
right, and get it done right now."

"He's a smart man to build a town this size,"
Morgan said. "He must have some other ideas
how to win the argument."

"Indeed, he does, but he thinks this will
cement the city so strongly behind him that they
won't allow the road to go to the mountains and
bypass La Grande."

"What haven't you told me?"

"When Mr. Merriweather dies, his will states
that everyone now in town who owes him money,
will be cleared of that debt. Any property being
bought by individuals will be conveyed to their
ownership with no more payments, and those
renting buildings or property directly from Mr.
Merriweather will become the sole and legal
owners of those properties and businesses."

"I'll be damned," Lee said softly. "The old goat
is buying a whole town's loyalty."

"No, just half the town. But with thirty or forty
strong movers to get the rail line here, he's sure
that we can out vote and out push Wert and his
team."

"You'll be taking over the Gunsmoke Saloon, I'd guess," Morgan said to Ormley.

"Why . . . yes, that's true."

"Who else knows about this plan?"

"Only Mr. Merriweather, his lawyer and myself."

They kept talking.

Later, they had another cup of coffee and a piece of pie.

The owner came to close up and they moved to the hotel owned by Mr. Wert. They went on talking in hushed tones.

"Mr. Merriweather would prefer a heart shot when he's sleeping in his chair, if possible. That way he'll look nice in the coffin."

They talked for another half hour and at the end of that time Morgan stood up and they went outside.

"When can I tell Mr. Merriweather that you'll do the job?" Ormley asked.

"You can't, because I won't. The whole thing stinks. It's a set up. He not only wants to be dead, he wants a hanging for the man who kills him. He's a selfish old bastard. Forget you ever saw me. I'll be out of town in the morning."

"But, I was so certain . . ."

"Then do the job yourself and pay yourself the thousand and become the owner of that run down saloon." Morgan turned and walked away.

He felt better, but not much. What a stupid idea. The old man was going crazy. At least Morgan still had most of the sixty dollars. He put his roan into the livery and she watched him as he unsaddled her.

"Don't get too relaxed here, old nag. We won't be staying that long."

On his way back to the middle of town he passed a store that had some kind of machinery running, a clanking and grinding, followed shortly by a clatter and then one of the roughest string of swear words he'd heard in days. They all came through a window and were definitely from a woman's mouth.

He went a dozen feet down the alley and looked into the window. Inside, four lanterns lighted the back shop of a newspaper. A woman sat on the floor beside a hand throw press and went right on swearing. A printer's form filled with type lay on her legs and she didn't seem to be able to get up.

"Front door unlocked, Miss?" Morgan asked through the window.

She stopped swearing, brushed a tear back from her cheek and smudged it with black printer's ink.

"What?"

"I could help you if the front door is open."

"Locked, try the back door."

A few moments later he walked up beside her and lifted the dead weight of the full newspaper form off her legs. She wore blue jeans and a blue shirt that was not tucked in.

"Can you get up?" he asked.

"Hell yes, nothing's broken. Who are you?"

"Lee Morgan, just passing through."

"That's the trouble in this town. Most everybody is just passing through."

"Tough newspaper town?"

"It's a no-no newspaper town. No circulation and no advertising." She held out her hand and he lifted her to her feet. "Charlie is the name. Charlie Kelton. Really Charlene, but you call me that and I'll kick you wherever I can reach."

He shook his head.

"I run this almost-newspaper, the La Grande *Observer*. Founded 1863, now with the proud circulation of just over a hundred and fifty, and most of those are used to wrap up garbage before burying it."

"Sounds about right," Morgan said. "This Wednesday?"

"Yep."

"Press day. You want that page form put in the press or is it going to sit here and grow mold on it right where it is?"

"I can do it myself," Charley said, moving to the form. Morgan held it with one hand and pointed at the press.

"What's head up on this thing?"

"You a press man?"

"Nope."

"Good, 'cause I do the whole damn paper by myself. I get the news, I write it, I set it in type, and I print it."

"Hooray for you. How many pages?"

"Four this week, that's cause I sold enough advertising for two pages."

"Sounds about normal." He put the form in the press, locked it in place and made sure it was all registered right. Then he took a wood block and a mallet and gently tapped over the face of the type to be sure none of the individual letters or spacers or column rules had worked up. It was the front page.

"You gonna put some ink on that or just let it run through dry?" Morgan said.

"I can ink it," she said.

He watched her use the ink roller and ink the

whole front page. She was feisty as a mountain lion, about five-feet one, and dark haired and dark eyed. Morgan decided she was as cute as a fawn prancing in the woods just after a spring rain.

She inked it and put on a sheet of newsprint. Morgan caught the handle of the big counter-weight and brought it forward, pushing the heavy cushion down against the paper and printing the sheet.

She put another piece of paper on and he moved the heavy press handle again. After four sheets she had to ink the page again. As she did she looked at him.

"You ready to do that about three-hundred more times?" he asked.

He saw that one side of the page was blank. "If you have a page two we better do it about twice that many. Is page two ready?"

"Yeah. Where you learn about newspapering?"

"Wound up broke and out of work one winter in Colorado. Instead of starving to death and freezing my . . . my nose off, I worked at the little weekly paper and print shop."

"Lucky for me." She watched him again. "You don't aim to be paid for this, do you?"

"No, ma'am. Nothing but a smile and a thank you. And maybe some information about this booming town and the railroad and all the fuss."

"Done," she said, then flipped another sheet of newsprint on the press and positioned it. Soon they had it down to a routine and a rhythm.

It was after ten o'clock before they were done printing.

"In half an hour they'll be dry enough so I can collate them and fold. Then I'll be done."

"No door to door delivery?"

"Let 'em come and buy them, if they want," Charlie said. "When I get up the gumption, I do deliver them door to door . . . ."

"Why not tonight when you've got some free help?"

Charlie looked at him, her face serious. The smudge of ink on her cheek had grown with two more smears and strands of dark hair straggled down from her forehead. More had spilled out of a band at the back of her head which held the long locks. Slowly she smiled.

"That's a smile that could whip a whole outlaw band," Morgan said softly.

"Lee Morgan, I don't know what you're after, but whatever it is you won't get it here. I'm more than glad for your help, but I can't pay you . . . with anything."

"No payment needed, just another smile now and then."

It was nearly eleven when they had the papers all assembled and folded twice. They looked at the stack and she brought two cardboard boxes to put them in.

"Ready for a walk in the moonlight?" she asked.

They walked the town, pushing papers under merchant's doors, leaving a stack here and there for firms to sell to customers.

Then they walked the back streets and pushed a paper on the stoop or porch or steps of every house in town.

It was just after one A.M. when they finished. There was a gleam of sweat on Charlie's smooth brow. She looked up at the tall man beside her.

"I could do with a shot of whiskey and some

branch water. What about you?"

"Sounds good."

"My place. I have some rooms in back of the newspaper. Cheaper than buying a house, too."

The three rooms were set up like a neat apartment. The kitchen was small, near a good sized living room. She didn't show him the third room which must be the bedroom.

Charlie took a bottle and two glasses from a cupboard, then poured water from a gallon jug.

She pushed the fixing toward him and Morgan put two fingers of whiskey in the glass and passed on the water.

She put the same amount of whiskey in her glass and doubled it with water. She lifted her glass.

"To a fine job. Thanks for the help. At those wages, I should put you on steady every Wednesday night."

"As long as I'm in town," he said.

They touched the glasses and drank.

She told him about how she had learned the newspapering business at her father's side, and when she got a surprise inheritance of five thousand dollars from an old aunt, she decided to come West and start her own paper.

"Two years, I've had the *Observer*. Not making any money, but the doors are still open."

"You'll make it," Morgan said. He stood, put the empty glass down. "Thanks for the town's history. I might stick around awhile, I'm not sure. Sounds like things could be happening."

"Don't forget . . . ."

He nodded. "Next Wednesday night, about six." He turned and went out the door of the rear entrance to the print shop.

Morgan was halfway to the faint lights of the saloons on Main Street when he saw shadows beside him. Two of them. He stabbed for his six-gun as a shot blasted almost in his face. He felt one of them kick his holster and his hand sending the weapon out of leather and into the dust. There was no time to find the Colt because the two were on him, knives flashing in the pale moonlight.

One hand grabbed his shoulder and spun him around. They hesitated a moment, knives ready, a pair of experienced men who knew how to kill a man quickly and silently. Morgan figured they probably enjoyed their work.

Chapter Three

Lee could hardly see the two dark shadows that closed in on him again, confident now that his gun was gone, figuring that he wasn't a knife man. There was no time to get at the sticker in his boot. For a second Lee relaxed, totally. Then he exploded forward before the pair could attack again.

A big blade came out of the dark, slicing into Lee's left arm, bringing that jolting pain of raw steel cutting flesh. He gasped, then saw the opening and his right elbow jolted out and rammed hard into the closest killer's sternum. The smashing blow drew a cry of pain from the knife man as he sagged to the left. Lee stepped forward with his right foot following through after the elbow smash and kicked with his left foot. The toe of his boot drove toward the second knife man's crotch, grazed past his thick thighs and powered upward.

The force of the kick smashed one of the attacker's testicles into jelly against his pelvic bones. The man roared in pain and fell to the ground, grabbing his crotch gently as he curled into a protective ball. Lee heard the big knife hit the dirt. He saw its blade glint in the soft moonlight and grabbed the handle.

It was a man's knife, a Bowie with double sharpened four inches of tip and a blade eight-inches long. Lee swung it and liked the feel.

He whirled as the elbow punched man gained his feet and stormed after Lee. The attacker came in a dark shadow blur, arms, waving, half spoken vile words on his lips as he drove forward for a sure kill.

By the time he got there, his target had moved. Lee kicked one of the attacker's boots into the other one, pitching the man into a stumbling sprawl on his face in the dirt of the alley.

Lee dropped on him, his left knee in the middle of the man's back, driving him flat into the dirt. The tip of the heavy knife sliced an inch wide line of blood across the downed man's forehead.

"Who sent you after me?" Lee demanded.

"Go to hell!"

"Undoubtedly, but not within the next five minutes. Who sent you after me?"

"Your mother!" The man shouted it and tried to rise, but Lee lifted an inch and dropped all of his 185 pounds down hard with the battering ram knee into the man's back. The knifer cried out in pain and then swore.

"Nobody sent us. You looked like we could get a couple of drinking dollars off your body."

"Nice try." Lee sliced the big blade down the man's cheek, bringing a gout of blood and a scream of pain.

"Who sent you after me? Every time you lie, I cut you. I've got all night."

"The boss, guy who runs the town."

"Merriweather?"

"Hell, no. The other one, Mr. Wert."

Lee saw the first attacker limping off into the darkness. He let him go. He wouldn't be a threat for a couple of days. Lee stepped back from the blob in the dirt.

"Get up," Lee said. The man looked up at him, then rose cautiously, watching the man with the deadly Bowie who loomed over him in the pale moonlight.

"Name?" Lee demanded.

"Don't make no difference," the man said as he watched the larger man. "No difference at all." He pulled a derringer from his back pocket and almost got a shot off before Lee sliced down with the Bowie. The heavy blade cut to the wrist bone on the gun hand and continued downward breaking both bones and brought a roar of agony from the knifer.

Lee pulled the knife back and drove it forward. It stabbed upward below the rib cage, plunged in to the hilt and then Lee roared and tore the big blade out the other way slicing six vital organs in half. The man's eyes went wide in the pale light. His voice came as a whispered protest, then blood spewed from his mouth and he fell toward Lee.

Morgan sidestepped the dying man, looked over his shoulder and watched him crash in to the dirt.

The feeling that swept over Lee was familiar, so heady, so enticing, so enthralling that he stood there savoring it. There was something about killing a man that jolted his senses right down to the raw nerve endings. It was an experience that both fascinated and horrified him, but it was there, a cloying, manic touch of insanity; a glorious life or death triumph in combat, a rush of feeling that came in no other way and left him drained, gasping for breath and wondering how life could produce another surge of emotion to top this one.

Slowly the rush ebbed, his breathing slowed and his eyes narrowed from their wide-open fascination. He panted for a moment, then rolled the body over looking for any identification. Nothing, not a note, a purse, a slip of paper, a hotel key. Nothing. He picked the man up and carried him two blocks over, dumped him in some weeds, and then wiped the heavy Bowie blade on the dead man's pants and pushed the knife into his boot.

Only then did he look at his cut left forearm. His shirt sleeve had soaked with blood. He needed some repairs. Morgan went back to the scene of the fight near the newspaper office and searched until he found his Colt. He checked the action, dusted it off and put it back in his holster.

Then he went through the rear door of the newspaper. Charlie sat under one lantern checking the front page. She looked up. "Didn't I hear a shot outside?"

"Yep."

"And you're hurt! Come over here and let me look at that arm."

Ten minutes later she had stopped the bleeding, cleaned off the blood and bandaged the cut, a nasty slice three inches diagonally across his mid forearm on top. He'd live.

"Thanks," he said watching her closely.

Charlie smiled. "Lee Morgan, you are a strange cuss. You have the manners, the words, the style of a gentleman, but you show up here looking like a worn out, used up, grub line rider who had given up on life." She watched him. "You mind a lady giving you a suggestion?"

He shook his head. The let down after the fight hit him full force. He shivered. It always came after the high, and now he could barely lift his hand.

"My suggestion is that you come up to my apartment and that I heat up some water and you have a bath. You own any clean clothes?"

Lee shook his head. He'd lost his carpetbag and blanket roll somewhere out of Portland to a trio of snatch and run artists. He couldn't chase all three of them.

"You don't sound enthused about taking a bath."

Lee looked up at her. She was cute as a speckled bug on a tulip. "Don't want to put you out any," he said. "Staying alive the past month has been a lot more important than staying clean."

She caught his right hand and led him down the shop carrying the lantern.

"Maybe I didn't make myself clear. I intend to *give* you a bath, not just let you scrub yourself." She looked closely at him. "Been a time since I scrubbed a man's back, but reckon I remember how."

"Then I scrub your back?" Lee said, working up some interest in the plan.

"If you'd like, and I sure hope like hell that you

will like."

Lee nodded and they went up the stairs to the second floor apartment.

She talked as the water heated on the wood stove. She told him how she started the paper, and had kept it going, but was losing money on it. "I can afford to lose another five hundred dollars. I'm close with my cash, so I should last another eight months. Then if things don't pick up, I'll have to sell out."

The water was ready.

She unbuttoned his shirt and took it off him. He undid his pants and dropped them.

"Oh, yes!" Charlie said softly. "Nothing is more beautiful than the pure form of a naked man. Not just his pecker, the whole body, torso, buttocks, waist, powerful back and shoulders and that chest. Delightful, beautiful!"

He stepped into the small galvanized tub and sat down, crossing his legs. He hated these little things. She washed him, being careful of the bandage on his arm. She played no favorites but did linger over soaping his crotch and when his penis boiled up with a surly erection, she giggled.

"About damn time," she said, and unbuttoned her shirt and dropped it on the floor. There was no garment under it. She stepped out of her pants and then took off some frilly underthings that were lacy and soft and tight.

She dropped the panties and stood there watching him where he sat in the tub.

"I had a bath last night," she said. She reached for his hand and waited for him to stand, then grabbed a towel and dried him. She grabbed his hand as they walked into the bedroom.

Lee had recovered and now he grinned. "You

sure about this?"

"I'm a grown up lady. I get to do what I want to do, for as long as I can." She stopped, smiled her prettiest and turned around slowly for him like a dancer.

"Do you like what you see?"

She was compact and slender with full breasts that seemed larger on her thin frame. A muff of brown hair swept down to her crotch as she stood sedately before him.

"Beautiful," he said. "Yes, I like every marvelous pound and inch of you."

She lay down on the bed and held out her arms. "Then come and convince me of it." She laughed softly. "Goddamn, it's been two years. Think I've forgotten how?"

Lee lay beside her. He reached out and kissed her lips softly. "If you've forgotten, I'll be more than pleased to give you some highly personal instructions."

"Show me."

He pulled Charlie on top of him, eased her down to his lips and kissed her quick and hard. His hands massaged her sides and back, then down to her bottom where he kneaded and gently slapped her.

"Oh, was I a bad girl? I like that. Spank me some more!"

The slaps turned into tender touchings, then he lifted her up and brought her forward until he could lower one breast into his mouth.

"Oh, dear man, yes! I'd forgotten how good that feels. I'm all mush and swooning and fainting and playing the maiden already. I'm glad I didn't know you when I was fourteen and so curious about what it would feel like to have a boy playing with my titties and my muff and showing me his body. A dozen times I thought I would explode."

He moved to her other orb hanging full and sweet into his mouth. Tenderly, he bit her nipple until it hardened and swelled and reached down proud and tall.

"Oh, god, I'm in heaven. Why do I ever say no? Course lately that hasn't been very often . . . nobody's been asking." She reached between them until she found his hardness and lay it precisely so it pushed at her crotch.

"Yes, glory! So near and so big and demanding. Oh . . . oh here it comes . . . . lordy, lordy . . . oh . . . ram me!"

Her body spasmed into a series of shaking, rattling vibrations that rocked her from chin to toes as she climaxed once, then twice, then twice more before she at last sighed and melted down on top of him.

"Oh, lordy!" she said, gasping for air. "What's it going to be like later?"

"Better," he said, pushing her on her back and kissing her breasts, then his mouth moved lower and she gasped as he invaded the soft brown hair over her heartland.

"You're not—I mean, it's all right—if you want to."

She shivered as his fingers parted the brown hair to reveal her nether lips. Morgan kissed the dampness there and her hips bucked upward into his face and Charlie climaxed again.

This time she moaned and writhed below him, shouting and squealing as her small body thrashed on the bed in one spasm after another.

When she trailed off, sweat beaded on her forehead. Morgan kissed her nether lips and sat up. At once she sat beside him, then bent and grasped his cock with both hands.

"Oh, my!" she said, eyes wide. Then slowly she bent and kissed the purple tip of him, and Morgan slowly humped toward her. She looked up at him, then opened her mouth and took him inside.

"Yes, yes," Morgan said softly. "I don't think you've forgotten a thing."

She growled at him and sucked him in as far as she could, then began bobbing her head up and down on him. She built up a rhythm and in a moment his hips were rising gently to meet her.

Then he caught her head with both hands and eased her off him.

"It's been too long for much of that," he said.

She kissed him and pulled him down on the bed on top of her. Charlie found one of his hands and brought it down to her crotch. His fingers began to explore. Soon he found the magic nodule and she gasped as he stroked it.

"Glory, glory!" she breathed.

A dozen times he rubbed across the node and she climaxed again, a long high wail that they both knew must penetrate outside but neither of them cared.

She came back to earth and grinned up at him.

"I'd say I'm about six ahead of you already. Don't you want to try to catch up?"

"Plenty of time," Morgan said. "I'd say we have all the rest of the night."

She looked at him in the dim light of the coal oil lamp.

"I'd say we have all night and maybe half the morning. Tomorrow is Thursday, the traditional day off of the weekly newspapering field.".

"You'll have me drained and worn out long before daylight," Morgan said.

"At least five times," Charlie said. She laughed. "Yeah, I'll be sore as hell tomorrow, but I haven't been sore for a long time." She lay on her back and spread her knees and lifted them.

"Hey, you, Lee Morgan. Right now. It's time. I can't wait any longer to see how that big stick of yours is going to feel buried about ten inches inside of my little cunny."

Before morning Lee found out he was wrong. He had lasted six times before they both collapsed on the bed and didn't hear the cock crow at dawn or again at six A.M. It was halfway to noon before they woke up.

Morgan looked over at Charlie, her long dark hair splayed over the pillow, a little girl smile on her face as she watched him.

"Fantastic," she said. "That is exactly why women get pregnant so often. They love to get poked."

Morgan laughed at the words out of the mouth of the innocent looking little lady.

"Probably a good thing," Morgan said. "Stay right there while I get breakfast. You do eat breakfast?"

"Usually." She sat up and her breasts bounced and swayed from the movement.

"Wonderful," he said and leaned down and kissed both her orbs. She kissed his hair in return.

"Wonderful yourself. Can you really fry an egg sunny side up and then drop it on a piece of toast?"

"Watch me."

They had eggs on toast and hash browns he fried up on the small kitchen range. Coffee and more toast and jam finished the meal.

Neither of them had dressed. The apartment had two windows but both were high up and posed no problem of exposure. She went to him and hugged him tightly, her hips pushing hard against him.

"Once more so I won't think I was dreaming last night," she said.

They made love again, quick and fast and hard and it left them both panting and gasping for breath. They lay apart on the bed staring at the ceiling.

"I could get used to this," Charlie said.

"I thought you were a career lady, dedicated to journalism and the American business ethic."

"That too, but I can still like my loving."

Morgan laughed. "I don't see why the hell not."

They both laughed and he reached for his pants. "First thing this morning is a haircut and a shave and then some new clothes."

"You're going to walk out and leave me with the dishes?"

"Ma'am, us working cowboys don't do no damned dishes."

She caught one of his hands and looked at it. There were no callouses, no rope burns, no rope scars.

"Cowboy? Not a chance. Not a single rope mark on you. Maybe a bank robber. That would be more fitting."

"Any money in the La Grande Home Bank down the street?"

"Damn little," she said and watched him.

"I'm getting used to that wild talk by now," he

said. "It loses its shock value if you use it too much."

She stuck out her tongue at him. He dressed and watched her doing the dishes, still naked.

"I like you this way, free and natural," Morgan said.

She turned to him, more serious now. "How many women have you made love to?" she asked.

"What?"

"How many? You're the third man I've been to bed with. I talk a lot but I never have . . . I mean, I don't actually do it much. Two years, damn!"

"Women are different."

"Not that different. I liked last night as much as you did. Now get out of here before I write an editorial about you." She grinned. "Also, I've got to get dressed—wear a dress. This is social and reporting day."

Morgan got the bloody shirt on and decided he'd get a new one first, then the shave and haircut. Right after that he'd go see that murder-for-hire-man, Slocum Wert, and have a nose to nose conversation.

Chapter Four

Morgan hardly earned a curious stare as he went to the Grande Ronde General Store and bought a new shirt. In this town, bloody shirts must not be anything unusual. He had his choice of lumber-jack plaid or cowboy tan. He took a tan that was nearly his size and had pocket flaps. He bought two pairs of pants and some summer underwear and headed for the hotel.

Morgan saw that it was aptly named for the owner, the Wert Hotel. He took a second floor side room, paid fifty cents a day for three days in advance, and went upstairs. After dressing in the new duds, he slapped the dust off his hat and put it on. It was the same wide brimmed, low crowned topper he'd had for over a year now. The black and red diamonds on the handband let him pick his hat out of a rack of them in a hurry.

Back on the street he found a barbershop and ordered a shave and a haircut.

"Cost you more 'cause you got a beard," the barber said.

Lee growled then nodded. "I never argue with a man with a straight razor in his hands." He knew it was going to hurt scraping off two weeks of whiskers, but he didn't remember it hurting quite this much.

The haircut was easier, trimming his locks to a neatness and letting his ears see the light again. The charge was seventy-five cents. Lee checked the cut in the mirror, nodded and gave the man a silver dollar and walked out.

Sometime early this morning in the afterglow of making love, Lee had thought of a solution to Rudolph P. Merriweather's problem. He didn't have to die to give away his property.

Lee walked into the Gunsmoke Saloon just as it opened at noon. The apron behind the bar was just setting up his glasses. The man led Lee behind the bar to the great man's office.

Merriweather sat behind his desk with a lamp beside a book he was reading. He looked up with a scowl.

"Yes, yes?" he squinted over half glasses. "Ah, Mr. Morgan. Glad you've decided to accept my proposition."

"Not at all, Merriweather. Why do you think you have to die to give away property, even money? You don't. All you have to do is sign the damn grant deeds and it's done, all legal and proper."

"Oh shit!" Merriweather said.

"Get rid of everything you want to, then take some of your money and go to San Francisco and see the sights, or get three whores in a room and let them use candles on each other. You aren't tied down to this little town."

"Oh, damn," Merriweather said putting down his glasses. "You don't know about Franny, do you?"

"Franny?" Morgan asked. "If that's someone in town I'm supposed to know, the answer is I don't."

"Yep, figured. You better have a beer, or better, about three shots of whiskey." Merriweather rang a big cow bell and the barkeep hustled in.

"Yes, Mr. Merriweather?"

The old man behind the desk chuckled. "Damn but I like good service. Tupot, bring me a bottle of our good whiskey, and three cold beers. Right now."

"Yes, sir, Mr. Merriweather." The barkeep hurried out.

"Fact is, you better hear about Franny and then meet her. Now that will be something." He stared at his door and a moment later Tupot came charging through with the drinks. Merriweather poured two shot glasses of whiskey and pushed one toward Morgan.

"Fact is, Mr. Morgan, Franny is my own flesh and blood, one generation removed. She's my granddaughter. She's twenty-two years old, pretty as a Spring fresh trillium, and about as pig headed as I probably was at her age.

"Her parents both dead and gone. My son wanted this high strung horse, and fancied himself something of a buggy racer. He'd take on a challenge from anybody.

"On the way to church one Sunday morning the three of them were prancing along in the buggy when a challenge was made, accepted and the race began.

"Nobody is for damn sure what really happened. Either the horse ran away and couldn't be stopped, or it was an out and out accident.

"Fact is, the buggy turned over and went down a little gully and killed my son and his wife instantly. Their young daughter, about ten at the time, survived without a scratch on her."

Morgan tossed down the whiskey and poured them both another as the old man talked.

"So there I was with a ten year old child to raise. No other kin, no other issue. She was my sole surviving relative. Spoiled that girl double rotten, saw to it that she got more education than any woman should get—two years at the university over at Eugene.

"She stayed in the house that now became hers. I saw that it was staffed with a cook and caretaker and all. Both her parents had some insurance and I could afford to spoil her.

"Now, she's twenty-two and thinks she owns the goddamn moon and stars. She's the reason I can't go to the lawyer and sign away a penny's worth of property."

Morgan shook his head. "I still don't understand. How can she control what you do?"

"Easy. A year ago I had a small stroke. I couldn't talk plain for a while and my left side took a rest for three months. During that time she went to the circuit court and got me declared incompetent to handle my own affairs. She was appointed my guardian.

"Yes, most of the restrictions are lifted, but she still has a firm veto power on all of my property. None of it can be sold or transferred without her signature.

"When she found out I gave a young widow her house free and clear after her husband was killed in the woods, Franny came in here with fire and steam and loud words. The deed of transfer was rescinded. Franny finally relented a little and the widow's house payments were delayed for a year."

"So she has you tied up over the property. What about your cash reserves?"

"Not enough to do any good. Thirty, forty thousand in stocks she forgot about. But I want to give away property, so I can get the folks in town enthused about the new railroad!"

"Wouldn't such an agreement also include property deeded in a will?" Lee asked.

"Nope! She forgot about that. Just that I couldn't sell or give it away. Checked with my own lawyer. He says she hasn't touched the will. She'd have to contest it, which my lawyer says he doesn't think would work.

"So, the will is my only way to get around her."

"Maybe I could have a little talk with Franny?"

"What you got against killing me?"

"Nothing, really, I just like twenty-two year old spoiled brats."

Merriweather grinned. "By damn, you just might get through her thick skin at that. Have a go at her."

"She lives here in town?"

"Indeed, the three story house just a block off Main at third. Has little dormers on the roof."

"Would she be home this noon time?"

"More than likely, unless she's gone to Portland to do her monthly clothes shopping."

Lee drank the last of his second shot of

whiskey and nodded. "Been good talking with you. See what I can do with this young lady you mentioned."

Ten minutes later he walked up the bricks to the front door of the fanciest house in La Grande. He started to ring the twist bell but the door opened.

A woman stood there staring at him. She had one delicate fist on her hip, the other hand caught in mid air after she let go of the door. The light blue dress would cost a working man two months pay. It was sleek, elegant. Morgan's first thought was *what a pretty woman!*

"Well . . . good morning. I'm looking for Miss Fran Merriweather."

"Yes, yes, that's me. And you are Lee Morgan who has been bothering my poor, sick grandfather. I'm putting you on notice right now that you are to leave that gravely ill old man alone."

He completely ignored her diatribe.

"Miss Merriweather, would you have a few minutes this afternoon for a serious conversation? There are several things we need to talk about."

She glared at him in surprise. Her mouth fell open and her expression indicated she did not believe her own ears.

"I just told you . . . "

Morgan picked her up with a sudden movement forward, dumped her slender waist over his shoulder and carried her into the living room.

"The house is beautifully done, Miss Merriweather," he said through her squeals and cries of fright. No one appeared to help her. Morgan came to a large upholstered couch and he gently sat her down on the sofa. He sat down beside her.

Fran sat there a second so mortified, so angry, so awe struck that anyone would have the nerve to do what this ruffian just did, that she couldn't speak. She swung her right hand to slap him.

Morgan saw it coming and caught her hand easily, then pulled her forward and kissed her lips. Her eyes went wide in surprise and fury. Then his arm went around her and crushed her to his chest. Slowly her eyes closed and she relaxed against him.

A moment later he released the kiss but still held her.

"Trickery and muscle, that's all you men think about."

"We don't slap from ambush."

"I didn't."

"You tried."

He felt her breasts warm through his shirt. She had made no move to be released.

"Franny, if I'm going to hold you so close this way, at least I should kiss you again."

She watched him from soft blue eyes. "I'm not fighting to get away," she said, a touch of a smile showing.

He kissed her again. She met his lips and the kiss was gentle then, more demanding as she pushed hard at his lips and began to part her own.

Morgan eased away and released her.

"Why did you stop?" she asked.

"I came here to talk, not to seduce you."

"You had the battle almost won."

She leaned back on the sofa and doubled up her fist and thrust it under her own jaw. A frown grew on her face. "You want to talk about gramps, right?"

"Yes. You know what he wants to do?"

"Yes, give away half of his fortune. It's all mine, will be as soon as he dies. He should have died three or four years ago. He had pneumonia and beat it. Noboby beats pneumonia."

"That's what I enjoy, a close, loving family."

"A point for you. He probably told you I'm spoiled."

"Are you?"

"Of course. Money to spend, no one to really discipline me from the age of ten. What do you expect? I'm selfish, jealous, go on spending binges, and I'm afraid every man who smiles at me wants my bank account, not my body."

"If they do they're jackasses. From what I've seen, you have a delightfully sexy body."

She smiled. "Thank you. At last a compliment. I should kiss you again but you might think I was the seducer."

"I wouldn't exactly fight you off."

She shook her head and her honey-blonde hair twirled. "No, we need to talk . . . first. Did grand dad send you over here?"

"Send? No, I wanted to meet you. You're making a mistake thinking your grandpa is not able to manage his affairs. Your problem is you don't like how he's doing it."

"I told you, he wants to give away half the property he owns."

"He worked for it, he earned the dollars to buy all that land and buildings. He developed it, nurtured it. Now he's trying to give something back to the community."

Her voice was small. "But someday it would be all mine."

"How much do you want? What you need is a husband, two kids, and another one cooking in the oven."

She tried to slap him again. He caught her hand easier this time.

"What, no penalty for this try?"

"That was as reward before, not a penalty."

He released her hand and she stroked his jaw gently. "I saw you when you first came into town. You were a mess. I like you much better this way."

"Good, so do I. But sometimes it's more important to stay alive than to stay clean."

She nodded, white teeth showing as she bit her lower lip.

"Your grandfather has hired me to kill him."

"No!"

"Yes. He offered me a thousand dollars in cash."

"That's terrible!"

"Why, Franny?"

"Because . . . he's . . . he's my grandfather, and I love the old codger. I don't want him dead."

"That way he could give away all of his land and property, if he wanted to. Your court order doesn't touch his will."

"He wouldn't!"

"He sent for an outlaw to do the job, only the guy got killed on the way here. I showed up and he thought I was the Abilene Kid."

"Don't do it."

"Why not? How can I earn a thousand dollars any easier?"

"Simple. I'll pay you twelve hundred *not to kill him.*"

"That won't work."

"Why not?"

"I've already turned him down. I'd rather talk

you into letting him give away half of his property, the mortgaged houses and businesses. That way, you both win."

Franny shook her blonde head. "Won't work. I asked the court to draw up an evaluation of his worth. Do you know what he's worth today, right now? The court said over two hundred thousand dollars in lands, buildings and properties, more than fifty thousand in stocks and bonds, and another ten thousand in various back accounts. That's over two hundred and sixty thousand dollars."

"Slocum Wert is probably just about as rich. You mean half of that wouldn't be enough for you to live on for the rest of your sixty-five years?"

"Well, yes, but that's not the point. I have to protect my grandfather from himself. His mind is slipping. He's childish sometimes. Once he didn't even know who I was."

"That was when he had the stroke. He's recovered almost totally. I'd say he's sharper mentally than more than 90 percent of the people in this town. He's completely competent to handle his own affairs. All you've done with your court order is stop an old man from making a lot of hard working people tremendously happy."

"Oh damn." She stood. "Come here, I want to show you something."

They walked through the expensively furnished house, down a hall with original oil paintings on the walls, up a staircase that was open and had a gleaming bannister. At the top the soft carpeting continued down a hall lit even during the day with two cut glass lamps. At the end of the hall she opened the door and he stepped inside.

"My bedroom," she said. She walked over and dropped down on a bed with four posts and a fancy silk and lace cover on the top. She patted the spot beside her, but Morgan stood.

"I'm not going to say that I'll take you on an all week romp on my bed and my body if you'll forget you ever heard of my grandfather. But I am going to say that I would be properly thankful and generous if you would stay around town and make sure that no gunslinger comes in and shoots my grandpa. I don't want him to die!"

Morgan stroked his jaw. "You want me to protect your grandfather so his will doesn't go to probate? And you don't want him to die? Sometimes, Franny, you are a little hard to figure out."

"No, you're wrong. I'm always damn hard to figure out. Most of the time I can't even do it myself. Oh, hell!"

She threw herself backward on the bed and began unbuttoning the bodice of her dress.

"Come here, big man," she said.

Morgan sat down beside her on the bed and watched as she opened the buttons, then lifted away her chemise and the tops of two petticoats. Then she sat up so her full breasts swung out. Her nipples were small brown buttons on full pink areolas.

Morgan bent and kissed each breast and heard her suck in quick gasps of breath. Then he stood and backed away.

"Delicious, delightful. I should accept both of your offers, but I can't. I am interested, though. How long has it been since you've had a good long talk with your only living relative?"

A tear seeped down her cheek. "Right, been too long. We need to talk, to be family again." She held out her arms. "Are you too busy that you couldn't spare a half hour right now?"

"Not too busy, just want to see how things work out between you and your grand dad. And I am overdue to see a man. Last night he sent two men to kill me. They came close. I don't like that, so I'll have a man-to-man talk with this worm."

"Bet his name is Slocum Wert," Franny said. "He probably thought you were working for Grandad."

Morgan watched her a moment more. "You sure make a picture sitting there that way," he said. "I'll remember that pose."

Franny smiled. "Lee Morgan you be damn sure to remember this pose. And know that any time you want to come back, I can strike the same picture for you—for starters."

Lee picked up his brown felt hat, touched his fingers to his brow and walked out.

Two men across the street saw him leave the house. They turned abruptly and began talking and motioning at the building near them.

Morgan walked the other way and then slipped down the alley behind Main Street. He hurried into the first saloon back door he found and walked through it to the street. He had lost the two men who were following him.

He wanted to see Wert, but he wasn't sure where his office was. Morgan walked down the street and wondered who to ask. He felt someone following him. Morgan turned quickly but saw only a boy, maybe fourteen, behind him.

Lee watched in surprise as the kid dropped his right hand to his side and whipped it upward as he started to draw a six-gun from a holster tied low on his thigh.

Chapter Five

Lee Morgan didn't believe it. A kid, maybe fourteen, was drawing on him. In the blink of an eye, Morgan's hand came up with his own six-gun, thumb pulling back the hammer smoothly, automatically, the muzzle leveling out in quick point and shoot aim at the kid's chest. It was reflex, pure and simple.

For a fraction of a second the lad wavered between life and death. Then the boy's hand slipped off the butt of the weapon and his hand came past the six gun entirely. He had tried to draw too quickly and missed the revolver. He snorted, said something to himself, and looked up at Lee with a big grin.

Morgan lowered his Colt .45, pointed it at the ground and slowly let the hammer down with his thumb from the cocked position. He slid the weapon in leather and took four long strides, grabbed the boy by the shirt front and half dragged, half shoved him down the side street for two blocks toward the wide open range before he let go.

"Son, I almost killed you back there. Never, *never, never* do that again. Don't even pretend to draw a six-gun on a stranger. I was about half an eyelash from pulling the trigger. If your hand had lifted that weapon out of leather you'd be dead right now."

The kid grinned.

Morgan slapped him hard, spinning him halfway around.

"You don't understand. A gun isn't a toy. The only reason to draw down on somebody is to kill them. *It's no goddamn game!*"

Morgan pulled his hand back to slap him again but the kid ducked and started to cry. Lee stopped.

"Damn, don't ever do that again!"

The boy looked up at Lee.

"How old are you, kid?"

"Fourteen, most near fifteen next month."

"What's your name?"

"Kid Texas, and I'm a gunfighter."

"Right now you're a dead gunfighter. Where do you live?"

"Down the other way."

"Let's go."

They had walked two blocks when Kid Texas looked up at Lee.

"You gonna tell my ma?"

"Damn right! If I don't, somebody's gonna kill you."

Kid Texas' eyes grew larger for a moment, then they laughed it off. "Not me, I'm Kid Texas, and I'm the fastest gun west of the Pecos."

"You know where the Pecos is?"

"Sure, I was born right near there."

"That a real six-gun you have?"

"Yep."

"Let's see it."

The kid took out his weapon and handed it to Morgan. It was a cut down .32 caliber, six-shot revolver. Lee checked to be sure. It wasn't loaded.

"Kid, never carry an empty gun, it could get you killed. I don't ever want to see you with a gun again, do you understand?"

The boy nodded.

"Your Ma home?"

"Should be. Dad's a logger. He's gone 'cept on weekends."

They walked up to a small house near the edge of the town. The boy went in calling to his mother that they had company.

A large woman with an apron on came from the kitchen. Her hands were white with flour.

Lee handed the revolver to the woman.

"Afternoon, ma'am. You've got to keep this weapon away from your son. He nearly got killed this afternoon." Morgan told her quickly what happened.

"A tenth of a second, ma'am. If his hand hadn't slipped past the gun butt . . . ."

The woman frowned at her son, then looked at Morgan. "He won't carry it in public no more. His Pa would bust it up with a hammer if'n he knew, but that ain't right neither. I'll see that the boy don't wear it no more out of the house."

Now Kid Texas looked less than his fourteen years. He slumped on a kitchen chair, his chin in his palms.

Morgan looked at him. "Kid, you want to learn to shoot, you do it, fine by me. Just no more nonsense about fast draw. That's what keeps getting people killed."

Morgan touched his hat with his fingers and walked out of the house. Now maybe he could find out where Slocum Wert did his business.

On his way back to the downtown block, Morgan saw the newspaper office. Charlie would know. Wouldn't hurt to read up on the last issue of the paper, either.

He walked in the front door. Charlie looked up from her editor's desk, the green eyeshade casting a strange pallor over her face.

She smiled. "Good afternoon!" Charlie fairly glowed with happiness.

Anyone watching her would know she made love last night. On some women it seemed to show, or maybe they wanted it to show.

She stood and he went over and pecked a quick kiss on her lips.

Charlie laughed softly. "Oh, yes, yes. That was so . . . so . . . delicious last night and this morning. I want you to come back tonight."

Her smile was so honest, so fragile. He hugged her and smiled.

"Tonight is a long ways off. First I've got a couple of things to do. Read last week's paper and ask you all you know about the feud between Wert and Merriweather."

"Read first, I want to finish up this story about the advance engineering crew that went through town so quietly yesterday that nobody but me knew they were here. They demanded it that way."

She went back to her pencil and paper.

Morgan read every word in last week's edition. Now he knew a little more about the town. The school district was forming and would have taxing powers as set up by the state. There was a city council but one member elected refused to take office and refused to resign. They were trying to figure out how to get rid of him legally.

There was nothing about Merriweather or Wert.

Charlie came up behind him and rubbed her hands over his shoulders. "Mind?" she asked.

"No," he said, turning and rubbing gently on her breasts.

She caught her breath. "Oh, damn! It doesn't take much to get me started thinking real sexy things!"

"Later. Where does Slocum Wert have his office?"

"In the bank, the only brick building in town, the strongest building in town. At the corner of Main and Grand Ronde."

"Been past there. Now what else should I know? How long has this battle been going on? What else has happened?"

She sat on the front of her desk, dangling her feet over the side. She still had on the dress she said she had to wear today.

"From what I hear, Merriweather came here first and homesteaded, or rather simply, land grabbed, in 1861 and then homesteaded the land in 1863 when it was legal. He put Main Street right on the edge of his homestead and invited anyone else to homestead the other side and build the other half of the town.

"Takers were slow. La Grande was mostly a gleam in Merriweather's eye back then. Things moved slowly. Then along came Wert and took him up on the idea and we had ourselves a town. Seemed that the first thing they needed in town was a general store and a saloon.

"Merriweather put up both and then when Wert came, they got together and Merriweather sold the other man his small general store and they moved all the goods across the street into a much larger store. The former general store became the town's first whore house. Six girls, count them, six!

"Then like you've heard, the place started to grow. We got more cattle ranchers and the lumbering began and now we're moving toward near a thousand people here."

"Along with seventeen saloons."

Charlie glanced up quickly. "Not true. We have only five saloons. I keep track pretty well on things like that."

She stretched and the bodice of the dress threatened to rip apart at the seams. Her arms went high and her breasts surged against the fabric.

Morgan watched and grinned.

"Are you really sure that you don't have time right about now to explore this dress? I mean, you've never taken it off me, don't know what's underneath."

She reached out and embraced him, her breasts crushing against his chest. Her kiss was long and lingering.

When her lips left his, Lee growled. "The damn sacrifices I make just to find employment around this town. Right now I've got to go see that man about a bushwhacking."

He pushed her back gently and kissed both her

breasts through the taut fabric. "But you two beauties stay at home and I'll be back to see you."

Charlie shivered when his lips touched the cloth over her breasts and then she sighed. "Hurry back, I'm not going to make much sense writing this story now, I'm afraid."

Lee waved and went out the door quickly before he changed his mind. He had been thinking about trying to buy a good black snake whip. He'd lost his in a quick dash out of a grove of trees near Portland. He felt half naked without it. Doubtful if he could find one in this town that had any balance to it. He'd check the general store.

Morgan walked staight to the bank. When he pushed through the front doors, he found the inside looking much like most banks. Two cages where tellers worked in a long partition across most of the bank. A desk at the side and another lower partition between the customers and the bank workers and officers. To the far side was a door with frosted glass in the top half with lettering that read: President Slocum Wert.

A young man sat at the front desk with an eye shade exactly like Charlie's. He worked steadily on a set of account books. When Morgan stopped in front of his desk he looked up, stabbing a finger on a column of figures not to lose his place.

"Yes?"

"My name is Lee Morgan and I'd like to see Mr. Wert. He's expecting me."

The young man nodded, and led the way to the president's door. He opened it and stepped in.

"Mr. Wert, a Mr. Morgan to see you."

Before there could be a response, Lee pushed past the announcer and walked into the office.

Two men faced him, one about five-feet four with a Prussian short haircut and heavy gray moustache. He looked to be slender and wiry. He had to be Wert. He was at least sixty-five. His dark eyes gleamed as he stared at Morgan.

The taller man beside him held a six-gun aimed at Morgan's chest. He was thick set, looked quick and competent. He was not the killer in the alley who got away, nor one of the two men who had tailed Morgan that morning.

"Mr. Morgan, I've been anxious to meet you," Wert said. "Please sit down, we need to talk."

"Wert, last night you sent two men to kill me, now you want to talk. You're a real bastard, aren't you?"

Wert sat down behind his big desk. "Young man, I could have you arrested for murder, you know that."

"Self defense. When two men come at you out of the dark with guns and knives, someone is bound to get hurt. You might have me arrested with paid for testimony, but never convicted. You said we needed to talk."

The small man peaked his fingers and looked through the empty spot. "Indeed we do. You are a talent that I could use. Yes, I have an opening in my organization now."

"Why would I want to work for you, Wert?"

"Because you're out of a job, down to your last sixty dollars that Merriweather paid you. I'm glad you didn't take up his crazy offer. That brat granddaughter probably offered you some kind of a deal herself. I can't offer you a sleek body like she has, but there are plenty of other girls in town."

"Just what work would I do for you, Wert?"

"This and that, bodyguard, a little power politics here and there."

"I'm not a hired killer, Wert."

"Plenty of those around. What I want you to do is work for me, and not work for Merriweather."

"So that's it."

"Plain and simple."

Wert looked up at the man holding the gun. The big guard holstered the weapon but remained where he was.

"The pay is three hundred a month and room and board at the hotel. But before you decide, I want to take you on a small trip along Catherine Creek and into the edge of the Wallowa Mountains. I want you to know something about what this argument, between me and Merriweather is all about.

"I've arranged for a basket lunch and my best coach with the new springs. We can leave at once, if you have no other important work."

"Yes, I'd like to see this area that's causing all the trouble. About that food, it sounds good, I missed my midday feeding."

A short time later they were in a handsome coach with leather cushions and heavy leather sling springs much like some of the good stagecoaches were using. The effect was to lessen the jolts and give the sense of a small boat at sea.

The pair of matched blacks directed by a driver moved out smartly to the east through the gentle valley, then turned south tracking Catherine Creek. The food in the picnic basket turned out to be sandwiches and still warm fried chicken, potato salad and an assortment of fruit along with a jug full of hot coffee.

Morgan ate hungrily, concentrating on the hot fried chicken and the potato salad.

By the time Morgan had satisfied his hunger, the small stream swung sharply east toward the blue distant upthrusts.

"We call them the Wallowa Mountains," Wert said. "They are high in spots, going to almost ten-thousand feet at Eagles Cap. They draw a lot more rain than most of the area around La Grande and consequently there is a fine stand of timber. Lots of white or ponderosa pine, and lesser stands of Douglas fir and spruce. The fir here is not as good as the fir farther west, and not as valuable as a lumber crop."

"You seem to know the lumbering business without much actual experience," Morgan said.

"Oh, we've been sawing lumber up here for over five years now. But it's a horse and wagon operation. We haul in the logs usually with a pair of yoked oxen, and saw it, then haul the lumber to La Grande. We have a limited market. Some we've hauled to Baker, but now they have a mill. What we need is the railroad so we can expand our market, sell to Pendleton, all the way down to Portland."

He swept his hand at the succeeding series of hillsides that worked higher and higher toward the skyline.

"The point is, Morgan, there's a million dollars worth of lumber on these mountains, and I own or control most of it. I want it turned into sawed boards that·turn themselves into greenbacks in my bank account."

"You think the railroad right here to the sawmill will make that much difference?" Morgan asked.

"Damn right! It'll make or break my operation. Say I have to haul the sawed lumber another twenty miles to La Grande. That would make my lumber more expensive in Portland than the local sawed boards. Got to think of tenths of a cent a board foot here."

The small creek they followed was full of spring runoff, and bounced and chattered and bubbled down the gentle slopes, splashed around and across a rocky bottom and swept on downstream as if anxious to get on toward the Pacific Ocean via the Grande Ronde River to the Snake and then the mighty Columbia.

As the faint road worked up into the foothills, it became less and less used. At last they pulled around a bend in the road, past the opening to a small valley, and Morgan saw ahead a spiral of smoke near a large wooden building and stacks of lumber that sat nearby curing in the sun.

The driver stopped the carriage.

"There she is, best damn sawmill in half of eastern Oregon. Damn fine operation. But it's going to hell in a bucket if I don't get the railroad out here!"

"You planning on logging just this side of the mountains?"

"Hell, no! There's a pass up there. Some of my biggest sticks come from over the crest. Once we get set up, I'll be able to afford to build a short line logging railroad right into the heart of the Wallowa Mountains.

"They extend about twenty miles across and maybe twice that long. Must be more than 800 sections of timber up here. And I'm the one who's going to cut it."

Morgan reached in the picnic basket and took the last leg of chicken out of the bowl.

"Yeah, I can see why you're so enthusiastic. Great country. Clean and pure. Not a lot of wood smoke fouling up the air. But what about all your stores back in La Grande? Won't they miss out if the railroad goes around them this way?"

"Not that much. We get everything in by wagon now. Won't change all that much. Don't make much difference to the stores, but to the sawmill it's life and death."

"So you want me to work for you."

"Indeed, that I do, Mr. Morgan."

"Just what will my duties be?"

"Like I said before, little of this and little of that. Don't worry about what you're to do. I'll let you know. Right now the biggest thing I want you to do is not to work for Rudolph Merriweather."

"That's all? Hell, sign me on. Oh, I'll need a months' wages in advance. I've had some expenses here."

"I'll get the money for you when we get back to town and talk to them at the hotel." Wert grinned like he had just won a big contest. "Damned if this don't make me happy. Got the jump on that damned Merriweather this time. Right now I'm glad you escaped from those two assassins last night. Yeah, damn glad."

Morgan could not have expressed his own feelings any better.

Chapter Six

When Morgan returned from his carriage ride, he collected his three hundred dollars in greenbacks and walked out of the bank with a broad smile. He felt the roll of bills in his pocket and smiled again.

Damned if he wasn't working for both sides!

No, not so. He hadn't signed on with Merriweather. Just counseled him a little. Hey, hadn't he turned down eleven-hundred dollars from that sweet, sassy little Franny? Damned right he did. He should have taken the money, bounced her in bed about four times, and ridden on for Boise. Should have done is not the same as doing.

For just a fleeting second he had a feeling that he was being followed. He turned and saw no one behind him. Nothing was going to spoil his good mood. He could get some more new clothes and a carpetbag to pack them in, and see if he could find a good black snake whip.

Morgan looked in the window of the general store and noticed a reflection of someone behind him.

The figure came toward him with an exaggerated walk. Damn, it was Kid Texas himself. He was trying to imitate the loose jointed, rolling gait that Morgan had been using. The boy stopped and stared at Morgan. Then he reached down and untied his holster rawhide and forced it lower on his leg, then tied it again. He pushed his wide-brimmed straw hat back the way Morgan remembered that he had done so many times.

The damned kid was copying every move that Morgan made. Morgan whirled and the youth had no place to hide this time.

"Hey, Kid," Morgan called pointing at the boy. "Over here."

Kid Texas touched his chest and Morgan nodded. He ran to where Lee stood and grinned.

"Follow me, Kid. I've got a job for you."

Morgan walked three doors down to the Wert Hotel, found a pad of paper in the lobby and wrote a note, then folded it three times and gave it to the boy.

"That's a message to the editor of the *Observer*. You know where the newspaper office is?"

"Yes, sir, Mr. Morgan!"

"Good. You take that to her and wait for a reply. I don't want you reading it, you understand. I'll know if you do."

"No sir, don't read it, and wait for a answer."

He started to leave but Morgan called him back. He fished a dime out of his pocket and tossed it in the air. Kid Texas caught it.

"That's for you. Now hustle that right over

there, and no loafing along the way."

"No sir, Mr. Morgan. Right away!" Kid Texas ran down the street toward the newspaper office.

Morgan wondered what Charlie would say when she read the note. He had written: *This kid has been following me around like a puppy dog. Can't you put him to work for a dime a day doing something? Be in your dept. (I'll pay the dime!) . . . . Morgan.*

He watched Kid Texas run around the corner. Good riddance. Lee thought again about what would be most interesting and perhaps produce some results for the town's dilemma. He went out the side door of the hotel and working the alley, soon found the big house on the corner where Franny Merriweather lived.

He knocked. She was home and invited him inside. She wore a soft blue dress that he was sure was expensive, beautifully made and dazzling. It also showed about half of each of her breasts. She twirled around and the skirt flared out lifting six inches off the floor.

"Like it?" Franny asked.

"Delicious," Morgan said. "The dress is nice to."

"Oh, you." She came to him and kissed his lips quickly. "I hope you had a good dinner because we're not going to eat anything until midnight. I gave the maid and the cook the night off, so we're all alone in this big house. We can run around naked and use any room we want to."

He caught her hand. "First, pretty lady, we talk. I'm worried about your grandfather. He tried to get me to kill him, remember? That gambler who runs the Gunsmoke Saloon might do it. He stands to own the saloon if he kills your gramps. Big temptation."

"If he did it I'd kill the bastard," Fran said.

"But it would be a little late. Your grandfather could hire any saddle tramp out of a saloon to do the job. Give him a hundred and he'd shoot and be gone. What I'm hoping is that we can work out a better solution."

"You were right about the will. I checked this afternoon with my lawyer here in town. We didn't think to include that in our list of situations we had covered."

"So, shouldn't we make a compromise with your grandfather? Let him have his way with some of the buildings, maybe the homes he's lent money on."

"Damn! It was all so simple. Now if he dies, I'll be to blame."

"That's true," Morgan said.

"Well, let's worry about it tomorrow. Right now I've got a lot sexier things on my mind."

"Like what?" Morgan said.

She walked up to him with a wiggle that left little to the imagination. Her hips ground from side to side, then humped forward a half dozen times until she was against him. The last time she humped, her hips hit his but not hard enough to hurt anything that was starting to get hard.

"I think I have an idea of what you mean."

She sank down to the living room carpet, her arms around his hips.

"Morgan, right here, right now," she said. "Am I being overly demanding?"

"Damn right," Morgan said and they both laughed.

He knelt down beside her. She turned on her back and spread her legs before pulling her skirt up to her waist.

"Hey, Morgan, sweetheart. Anything you see lying around that you want, you just help yourself."

He bent and kissed her lips, then pulled away and pushed the top of her dress down so her breasts popped out.

"Oh yes, now that is fine," Lee said softly. He went down on one breast, sucking a mouthful in and chewing on the tender flesh.

"I . . . I think he's getting the idea," she said. Franny moaned as he bit her growing nipples. "Yes, yes, yes!"

She pulled his face up to hers and kissed him, a long, hot kiss that drove her tongue between his opened lips and deep inside his mouth. When at last they both gasped for breath and broke the kiss, he went down beside her.

"Tell me about the very first time you found out about sex," Franny said. "I mean the first time you shot off out of your little pecker."

"You mean it?"

"Yeah. What happened? How old was she?"

"About thirty-five or forty, I'd guess. I was just over fourteen and climbing this maple tree in my back yard and I was straining and pulling up with my hands and legs and first thing I knew, I was shooting all over the inside of my pants."

"You knew what it was?"

"Sure, I'd heard the older boys talking and even tried to pump it off with my hand, but nothing happened. That was my first ejaculation."

"Jeeeze, what a cheat. You want to hear about my first?"

"Unless it's too painful."

"Oh, hell no. I still think about it. I was thirteen, hadn't had my first bleeding, my monthly, yet, and I was swinging in the back yard out here. Usually there was a nurse or a nanny or somebody watching me. Grand dad always had lots of people around.

"The delivery boy came from the general store with some vegetables for cook. Nobody answered the front door so he came around the side. He saw me just when my skirt flew up around my face as I pumped hard on the swing. He could see my legs all the way up to my crotch.

"He put the groceries down and motioned to me and he said he had something he wanted to show me. I'd seen him before. He was fifteen, I think. He pointed into the big woodshed we had to store our winter wood.

"Inside it was kind of dark but we could see good enough. He turned around and did something. When he turned back his pants were open and his pecker poked out. It was stiff and hard and four inches long and he grinned.

" 'You showed me your panties, I thought I should show you my pecker,' he said.

"I'd never seen one before. I got all warm and excited and I asked what could it do? He opened up his pants more so I could see his balls and he put his fist around his cock and pumped three times and spurted. He was so fast.

"By then I was getting all wet at my crotch and I said I guess it was my turn to show him something. I slipped off my little panties and lifted my skirt. I was getting some hair, but not much, and he just stared at my crotch and my little slit.

"He told me to sit down and I did and he pushed me on my back and lay on top of me. At first I was scared, but then he said it wouldn't hurt and he wanted to just try to see if it fit into me. He pushed my legs apart and went down and the next thing I knew, he slid right inside me. He wasn't very big, but neither was I.

"He got so excited that he pumped three times and shot inside of me. I didn't really feel a thing. It was like shaking hands, sort of. He panted and huffed and moaned and then he came out of me. He helped me to get my panties and then he buttoned up his pants and ran out of the wood-shed so fast I thought he'd take the back gate off.

"I sat there a while, decided it was neither good nor bad. I'd have to get older to find out if I liked having a boy do that to me."

Morgan had been massaging her full breasts as she talked.

Now she growled deep in her throat and rolled over on top of him. "Right now, sweetheart! Do me right now before I explode. I like it now. God, please!"

"With our clothes on?"

"Yes. Right this second!"

Morgan opened his pants. She grabbed his penis and moved slightly so she got into the right position, then she lowered onto his staff.

"Oh, my god! Oh, my god!" she wheezed as he lanced deep inside her. Suddenly, without any movement, she climaxed. It was a softly controlled rumbling that ripped through her. She chattered and panted, then her hips began to pound against his and she lifted and dropped on him a dozen times. The climaxes rolled from one into the next.

She got up on her hands and knees and began to ride his penis like it was a small pony. She galloped and cantered and then settled down to a steady pressure that pushed Morgan over the top.

He thought she would drain every bit of juice from him. Slowly she came to a stop and let out one last big sigh, then melted down on top of him.

Her breasts were a soft cushion between them. They rested for several minutes, then Franny lifted up and looked down at him.

"Not bad for a first try. I just wanted to be on top the first time." She pushed off of him and reached down. "Let's go up to the bedroom where the featherbed will be a lot softer on my back."

She reached up and kissed him. "This is going to be a wonderful night. Let's be careful not to fall asleep and waste any of our precious hours."

The second time they used her soft featherbed. Morgan almost got lost in the piles of covers, but at last hit the target that kept sinking away in the feathers.

After the third time she caught his hand and they ran down to the kitchen. She had the cook leave snacks for them; cheese and some crackers and wine, slices of hard bologna and pickles, and just-made walnut fudge.

They ate and drank the good white wine and then she pushed everything aside on the table and crawled up on it.

"Sweet Lee. I never use the kitchen table, not even for eating. Why don't we make this one of our firsts?" They were both still naked. Franny giggled. "It's kind of cool up here. Think you can warm things up?"

He could, without any trouble.

Midnight came and went. They moved up to a small rooftop area on the third story that had a floor and a three foot railing all the way around.

A telescope tripod stood there waiting.

"Daddy used to come up here and watch the stars."

They looked up. It was clear and cool. The stars seemed so close you could play jacks with them. She reached up but couldn't quite catch one.

She pointed to a shadow along the railing. It was four heavy quilts.

"You planned this," he said.

"Of course. Nothing happens by chance."

They spread out the blankets and she fell on them, then got up on her hands and knees. She looked at him.

"Since we're outside and the stars are so bright, and nobody can see us up here, I thought we could play doggie."

Morgan laughed. "Which one?"

"Sweetheart, either one you want."

Morgan knelt behind her and eased into her top hole.

"Oh, my god! My god, but that is different. Only the second time ever. I mean ever! Sweet . . . " She gasped and climaxed and Morgan bent over her, grabbing her large hanging breasts, massaging them as she shivered and spasmed until he thought she would shake to pieces. When she finished she cried softly, "So damn fantastic!"

Morgan eased in a little more. The tightness and the whole idea of it smashed into him and he shot his juices deep into the unfertile passage. Then they fell forward, she on her stomach, he pushing down on top of her and still connected.

A short time later she moaned and he slipped away from her and lay beside Franny on the blankets. He slid his arm around her and they were aware suddenly aware that it was cool outside this time of night.

Morgan looked at the cowboy's Waterbury. The pointer stars of the big dipper angled at the North star. The dipper itself was at a 45 degree angle to the southwest. He showed her the dipper and the position.

"When the big dipper pointer stars are where the nine is on a clock, it means the time is ten p.m. When it's at a 45 degree angle down, it's two a.m. When the pointer stars are down where the six is on a clock, it's four a.m."

"Let's go down and make some coffee," Franny said. "That last one was the best yet, but right now I'm freezing my titties off."

They had coffee and more of the snacks. An hour later they settled down in her big bed, both ready to go to sleep. She nestled up against his side, curled into a ball, one hand across his crotch holding his manhood.

"This is the best part about making love all night," Franny said. "I just love to go to sleep cuddled up to my man."

Before Morgan could think of something to say, she was sleeping. Good idea. Morgan drifted off slowly, still trying to figure out how to keep the old man alive, yet get some of the property to the people he wanted it given to.

Maybe tomorrow he'd think of a way. Maybe.

Chapter Seven

Henry "Kid Texas" stood in the yard behind his house. If he looked east he could see no sign of human life. There was only the broad expanse of the Grande Ronde River Valley that faded into the blue hills and the far Wallowa Mountains looming starkly high against the horizon.

He stood stiff legged for a moment, then shook his head and slightly bent his knees. His hands hung loosely at his sides. Then in a surge of action he whipped his right hand up, made sure he caught the butt of the .32 caliber revolver hanging out of his holster and pulled the gun free.

"Single action, single action," he scolded himself. "Stupid, you have to cock it on the way up with your thumb, just the way Lee Morgan does."

He shoved the weapon back in the holster and

tried again. He did it again and again. Sweat prickled his forehead. A drip seeped into his eyes. He slashed away the wetness and tried once more.

This time he got the weapon out of the holster but didn't get the hammer locked back in a position so he could fire. The next time he missed the butt and knocked the gun out of the holster on the ground.

"Bang, you're dead, cowboy," Kid Texas snarled at himself. He pushed the iron back in leather and tried it again.

This time he caught the butt just right, closed his fingers around it, pushed his trigger finger into the trigger guard and his thumb brought back the hammer until it clicked.

As he lifted the six-gun he did a point and shoot.

"Bang!" He thumbed back the hammer with his right thumb for a second shot. "Bang. You're dead, you sidewinder!"

Yeah, he was getting it. Kid Texas pushed the six-gun back in leather and hung his right hand below the gun butt. He watched the other gunfighter step around the outhouse and grin. Kid Texas watched the outlaw and the man's eyes told the story: a killer on the loose. Somebody had to go up against him.

"It's just you and me, Deadeye," Kid Texas said.

"Yep, draw whenever you feel right," Deadeye said. They were his last words.

Kid Texas jerked up his hand, caught the weapon, fingered the trigger and slammed back the hammer, all in one swift move. Even as he did the weapon came up and aimed at Deadeye's chest and the squeeze let the hammer fall. A half a second later, Deadeye Lacrosse slammed backwards into the dust of El Paso, dead in an eye blink with a .45 slug deep in his black heart.

Kid Texas holstered his six-gun and walked away. You always walked away from a guy you had just killed.

A voice broke through from the throng watching along the boardwalk. It was a woman's voice.

"Henry! Henry, come in here, please. I have an errand I want you to run for me."

Kid Texas shook his head and then looked up at his mother. What a comedown from just saving the town from Deadeye. Someday he thought, it just might happen, and hurried into the house unstrapping his gunbelt. His mom wouldn't let him go downtown wearing the gun anymore.

Morgan woke up at 6:30 as usual, slipped out of Franny's bed and dressed. Someone was working in the kitchen. He went out the front door without being seen and walked down to the Wallowa Cafe for eggs, bacon, country fried potatoes and a gallon of coffee. The girl behind the counter filled his cup again leaning over a little more than was necessary.

He had a look down her blouse top and caught a full view of her breasts, nipples and all. She grinned and leaned back watching him. "Anything else you'd like?" she asked, smiling.

"You bet, but not right now."

"Maybe later. You're new in town."

"True, but I enjoy two beautiful sights when I see them."

She laughed. "My name is Lara. You stop by near closing time."

"See what I can arrange." He pushed back, paid his tab at the counter and strolled outside.

La Grande began to wake up.

A farmer brought in produce for the general store. His wagon was loaded with fresh fruit and potatoes, carrots and a variety of baskets filled and covered.

The ice wagon moved down the street. The ice man carried twenty and thirty pound chunks of river ice in to coolers and ice boxes. The ice came from the ice house out on the ice pond that froze last winter. The ice had been sawed into chunks, then put in a wagon and hauled to the nearby ice house where it was stacked with layers of straw between it so it didn't freeze into one solid chunk. This ice house was dug halfway into the ground so the ice would last longer in the hot La Grande summer. Usually, by mid August when it was the hottest, the ice was used up. Somebody suggested they build another ice house to double the capacity. It hadn't been done yet.

Morgan strolled down the street. When the general store opened he went in and bought two more pairs of pants and shirts, a fancy vest, a set of long underwear for the winter time and three sets of short summer underwear. He pitched in six pairs of socks and three handkerchiefs and paid the tab. Then he bought a soft sided carpet-bag and folded everything inside.

After he dropped his new wardrobe off at his hotel room, he ambled down to the newspaper office. The *Observer* doors were open. He could hear someone swearing inside before he stepped through the door.

His footsteps inside the office stopped the string of cowboy-type profanity.

"Morning, Charlie," Morgan said before he could see her.

"Oh, it's you." Charlie let go with another half dozen choice expletives before she came out of the back shop. "I'm trying to set up for six pages and I don't have enough furniture for my ads. You see where I put those little blocks of wood when I tore down last week?"

"Afraid I wasn't here, Charlie. You can use line spacers from your type case."

She looked up surprised. "Thought you said you weren't a printer."

"I said I wasn't a press man, which is true. Learned a little about a back shop working in one for six months. Where's your page form?"

Morgan followed her to the make-up bench and saw that she had two ads with a lot of white space. She needed the oblong blocks of wood called *furniture* to fill in the blank spaces so nothing would print. The wood was an eighth of an inch below type high.

Morgan found some pieces of three-quarter inch pine sticks that were two inches wide. He grabbed a saw and cut up half a dozen chunks of different lengths and brought them to the make-up bench. Using the new wood mixed in with the oiled and seasoned hardwood furniture, they got the form filled solid, tightened and locked up.

Morgan tapped the type and ads down with a mallet and leveling block and looked up. "Anything else?"

She moved up close and kissed his lips. Her dark hair swirled around them for a moment, then she stepped back.

"How's the arm?"

"Oh, I forgot all about it."

"Good, it must be getting better. Let me change the bandage and put on some more of old doctor Charlie's wonder salve."

She led him back to a table piled with paper and sat him down. The slice on his upper left arm showed some signs of starting to heal. There were no angry red lines of infection.

"Good," she said, as she salved it and re-wrapped it tightly with strips of cloth two-inches wide that had been torn from a sheet. "Now you're good as new." She frowned. "I thought you were coming to stay here last night."

"I got busy on something else. Wert is trying to hire me to work for him."

"Oh? Then it isn't important that I saw you going into Fran Merriweather's house yesterday afternoon?"

"Yes, it's important. I'm trying to talk her into letting her grandfather give away some of his property. She's got a court order that prevents it."

"Any luck?"

"Not yet. Oh, this isn't for publication, right?"

"I guess."

"I hear something about a meeting this noon?" he asked.

"Yes, a special town hall meeting. It's about the railroad. I'm sure both Wert and Merriweather will be there promoting their plans for the best route."

"Should be interesting."

"No, it'll be a waste of time. Nobody will change their minds, and I'll have to cover it and then write the story for the front page. You going to help me print out tonight?"

"Sure. Oh, did Kid Texas come yesterday?"

"Yeah. We decided you were playing a joke on him. But he said he made a dime on the deal. He's a real fan of yours. He says you can do no wrong."

"He's been following me around."

"Can you hand set type?"

"Can a Reb sing Dixie? I used to do a bit of it. Where's the case? Eight point?"

She had him set type for a small story for the front page. Morgan hadn't been at a type case for two years, but he remembered where each letter was. He set the type, read it upside down and backward in the type stick, then locked it in and went and pulled a proof on the three-inch long story.

He found two wrong letters, corrected them and pulled another proof. Then he put the stick of type and the proof on Charlie's desk.

She looked up surprised. She scanned the story quickly. "Hey, you can set type. You're fast and you're good. How about marrying me and going partners on the paper here?"

"Sounds great but I can't afford to lose any money like you can."

Hell, I was afraid of that. Then work here and crawl into my nightgown with me about twice a week."

"Why not every night?"

"Every night is fine, for as long as you can last. I'd say you'd give out after three weeks."

"No bet," Morgan said laughing. "Right now I want to check on Gramps Merriweather and try to talk him out of this idea of getting himself killed."

"Hey, just a minute." She left her chair and

walked over to him. Charlie pulled his face down and kissed his lips hard, a wanting, needing admission. Then she rubbed his crotch. "Christ! but I wish I had a man like you around all the time."

He bent and kissed her breast through the loose shirt and felt at once that she wore nothing underneath.

She sucked in a breath and let it out slowly. "Now?" she asked.

"Later."

"Promises to keep. Remember that."

"I will."

He hurried out of the shop and on to the boardwalk. Then down toward the Gunsmoke Saloon half a block away.

Ormley wasn't at all pleased to see Morgan. "You didn't take the job."

"Not a chance. I've got a better plan."

Morgan walked behind the bar and back to the old man's office. He knocked on the door twice, then opened it and looked inside.

"Come in, come in. A man can't even take time out for a little nap these days. Got to save my strength for the big debate at the Town Hall meeting."

"Talking is better than dying. I had a long talk with your granddaughter."

Merriweather looked up and laughed. "Bet it lasted all night, didn't it? Franny always was curious about men. She would have made a great whore."

"I'm trying to talk her into letting you have half of your give away."

"Fat chance, young Morgan."

"No, a good chance. She's weakening. I want

you to promise me that you won't hire anyone to kill you for at least two weeks. We can have this all settled by then."

"Two weeks. Don't seem long to live, does it?"

"Damn sight longer than two seconds, two minutes or even two days. I'd say two, four, six, eight *years* would be better."

"Yeah, true. Sometimes I wonder."

"Then it's a promise? Give me your word that you won't get yourself killed for at least two weeks."

"Hell, why not. I've waited this long. Another couple of weeks won't hurt. You might be just the one to twist Franny's tit and make her let go of that court order. I've got another hearing when the circuit judge comes back, but he won't be here now until October. My lawyer says we should get the incompetency charge reversed by then."

"Good, now I'll get to work on Franny again. She's a tough one, reminds me a lot of you."

"God damn right! Same good stock. Tough, demanding and just as obstreperous as all hell in a basket."

Morgan waved and went out to the saloon. He called over Ormley who was in a game of blackjack with two men. "I just talked with Mr. Merriweather. He guaranteed that he would not try to hire anyone to gun him down for the next two weeks. I'm holding you responsible to see that nothing happens to him. Let me put it this way, Ormley. If anything happens to Mr. Merriwether, a broken arm, a shot in the heart, a hangnail, the same damn thing is going to happen to you. Understood?"

Ormley's eyes went wide. He stepped back and

tried to speak. He shook his head. "I . . . I can't guarantee . . . I mean, he comes and goes . . . I can't just . . . ."

"Make sure you do, or somebody does. The old man stays alive for two weeks, or you don't. Simple."

Morgan turned and walked out the door. If the gambler had a gun, Morgan knew he'd be too cowed to use it. Morgan was right.

He went to the general store for the second time that day and this time bought a box of .45 rounds. He always liked to keep a few spares handy.

When he came out, the Town Meeting was starting on Main Street. Two farm wagons had been rolled together and the horses unhitched and driven away. The mayor and three members of the city council were already on the rustic platform. At the stroke of noon, the mayor held up his hands for quiet.

"Men. Men!" he shouted. The mayor was a man with little hair, a pot belly and red suspenders. He looked around, saw a sprinkling of ladies in the gathering, and tried again.

"Ladies and gentlemen!" his voice boomed. He repeated the phrase and most of the voices quieted.

"Time for the Town Meeting. I didn't want it, but I got my arm broken off, so here we are. The question before the house is should we ask the railroad to come directly through La Grande, or urge the tracks to swing east of Mount Emily and come down alongside the Wallowa Mountains?

"First to speak will be Mr. Slocum Wert."

There were a few good natured calls and a boo or two. Wert was grinning when he came up on the wagon. Two big men standing nearby lifted Wert up and tossed him on the wagon box.

"Without the assistance of men like these two, where would I be today?" Wert boomed out.

"Still in the street with the rest of us!" someone shouted, and everyone laughed.

"Rightly so, because I am a man of the streeets. Like the rest of you, I work hard every day, I know what it's like to sweat and strain. That's why I'm pushing for the eastern route past Mount Emily and down the Wallowas.

"Sure, I've got an interest out there. That's where half the jobs in this county are going to be in five years. Half of them, if the railroad goes that direction. Yes, that will mean a direct route to Pendleton and to the Columbia River and barges down all the way to Portland."

"How you gonna get past the falls there at The Dalles, Slocum?" a voice asked.

"Hell, unload and wagon the lumber around. River traffic is far, far less expensive. Or we could leave the lumber right on the train and drop ship to The Dalles, and at every town between here and Portland!"

"You gonna make yourself rich that way, Wert." Somebody called. "Why in tarnation should we make you any richer?"

A dozen voices lifted in agreement.

"Why?" Wert thundered. "Because I'm going to produce high paying jobs, jobs for the likes of you that ain't got one. Jobs for new people that will make your cash registers here in La Grande ring louder than ever before.

"With the railroad out there in the Wallowas, La Grande has the chance to grow into a city of twenty, maybe even thirty thousand souls.

What's that going to do to property values, to the first stores to take root here? Boom them, that's what it will do."

The mayor stood up and shook hands with Wert and looked at the crowd.

"One man's opinion. Now here's another man's opinion, Mr. Rudolph Merriweather."

Someone had put apple boxes down at the end of the wagon to make steps and Merriweather was helped up the rickety affair to the wagon bed. He nodded his thanks.

Morgan saw that the old man was unsteady on his feet and soon someone handed up a heavy cane that he leaned against. He looked out over the crowd nodding to people.

"Came here first in Fifty-Nine. Liked the looks of the place and came back in Sixty-One and started the town. Called it La Grande because I'd never seen anywhere so blamed beautiful. Been doing a mite to help the town grow ever since.

"Just doing my duty to the town, the county. Yep, I've made a couple of dollars, but I think you'll agree that I earned them. So now the railroad. I've seen railroads split up and ruin more towns than I can count. Sometimes a railroad goes eight, ten miles out of the way just so it can go through a town or a spot where the railroad sold some land or where somebody helped the railroad and now wants to be repaid.

"Don't let it happen here. Best route is west of the peak we call Emily. It should go through the Kamela Pass in the Blue Mountains this side of Pendleton, along the Grande Ronde and into La Grande. Best route, cheapest route, and it will serve all the people of La Grande, and not just one man building a sawmill!"

There were stamps of feet on the boardwalk and a chant in the background.

"You tell him, Merriweather!" somebody shouted.

"Sure, a big sawmill up there would be good, and will come in time, but first we take care of the most people, then we work on the one man and his sawmill. When time comes for the straw vote, I'm hoping you go with experience here and pick the La Grande route."

He stopped and the crowd cheered and the mayor took his hand and had others help him down.

"You heard both sides," the mayor said. "Now I want you to vote. First give an aye for all who want the Wallowa route."

There were shouts of aye scattered throughout the audience that had grown now to over two hundred people.

"Let's hear same sign, aye, for all those who favor the La Grande route."

The thundering chorus of ayes was far greater than the first vote.

"Straw vote is in favor of the La Grande route. We'll be having some railroad men through town in the next few days. Act real friendly and give them a fine La Grande welcome. Meeting is hereby adjourned."

Chapter Eight

Lee Morgan drifted away from the Town Meeting as it broke up. He ambled along with nothing to do and loving it. He could stand a little slow time for a while, now that he had money in his pockets. He'd made as much in a month here as he could working all year eating dust and getting rained on as a cowhand.

He looked at a display of new western hats in a store window, then took off and looked at his own hat with the red diamonds on the black head band. Yeah, good for another year or so.

Up the street he came to the bank and he walked inside. There were six customers there now after the big meeting. More people in town today then usual. Anybody could voice his vote in a Town Meeting.

He looked at the door to President Wert's office. It stood open. He walked over and stepped inside. Wert looked up from a paper on his desk.

"Just relax, Mr. Morgan. Nothing special for you to do right now. I'll be in touch."

Morgan nodded and left without saying a word. Talk might be cheap, but Morgan didn't feel the need to spend any more coinage on verbiage than was needed.

Ten minutes later he wandered into the *Observer* and looked around. The top of a black head showed over the big desk that was scattered with papers.

"Be with you in a second," Charlie said as she went on penciling on a news story. She finished and looked up.

"Hey! Great! Just the man I'm looking for. Want to practice your typesetting again? I need this story set for the front page. It's about the big Town Meeting and the railroad men due in town tomorrow."

She held up the story. It covered two pages of yellow lined paper. "I could always think of some nifty ways to reward you." Charlie smiled, stood and walked toward him.

A woman came in the office just then to buy a paper. She took last week's, paid her nickel and left.

Charlie approached Morgan like a big cat stalking her prey. At last she pounced and caught Morgan and hugged him tight, then held up her face to be kissed. When Morgan made no move, she reached up and kissed his lips hungrily.

"Was that a yes, or a no?" she asked.

"A yes, couldn't you tell?" He took the story from her and headed for the back shop.

Charlie watched him, her dark eyes glowing. "Hey, thanks. I'm a little behind today."

It was after four that afternoon when Lee Morgan dropped the last stick of type into place on the front page form and tapped it all smooth with the wooden block. He tightened the expandable metal chucks so none of the type could drop out, then tapped it down flat again on the marble slab topped make-up table.

"Got the damn thing done again," Charlie crowed. "Every time I get that last page made up I give a cheer. Never know if there'll be another one. We're heavy on ads this week, but still just four pages. Before I do six again somebody's going to have to pay for it."

"By damn!" Morgan said, grinning at her.

"Yeah, right. By damn!" She looked at the wind up clock ticking away on the table. "Hey, we didn't have any dinner. Least I didn't. Want something to eat before we print?"

"What's this 'we' stuff, woman. Did I sign on for the whole publishing process?"

"You signed on for whatever you want to do, cowboy. That means on the paper or in my bed. Which includes right now if you've got a wild beast in your pants pockets there."

"Hey, I never get hard up. Let's have something to eat. I did miss my lunch as the Eastern dudes call our noon meal dinner time."

She fed him cheese sandwiches and thin slices of fresh, locally grown tomatoes. Charlie put things away, then looked at Morgan who sat on her couch. She sat beside him.

"I need a couple of hugs," she said in a small, soft voice. "You have any to spare?"

He put his arms around her and held her. He kissed the top of her head and made sure his hands did not touch her breasts. She took a long breath and relaxed.

"This feels so good, Lee Morgan. Feels like you belong right there, and I should be here, and you just ought to be holding me this way. Am I being silly?"

"No, not at all."

"Sometimes I act kind of rough and swear a lot, but that's mostly just . . . a defense. I'm afraid people will see the real me and maybe not like me."

"What's not to like?" Lee said and kissed her neck.

She purred deep in her throat. "Nice. Not sexy, just nice and soft and tender. I certainly do wish . . ." She stopped suddenly and sighed again.

Morgan didn't say a word. He knew what she wished. He'd had a wish or two that way during the last few years. The wanting to settle down, to stop roaming, to find a nice little spread he could buy and go back to raising horses the way his dad William "Buckskin" Frank Leslie had done up on the Spade Bit in Idaho. But dreams like that didn't have much to do with reality.

He couldn't afford to buy a ranch. He couldn't afford to buy the breeding stock he would need to get started. Most of all, he wasn't sure that he could afford to stop and stay in one place that long. There were still some wanted posters out on him and some damned bounty hunter might come looking. Then too, he hadn't found the one woman he would want to settle down with.

She turned and looked up at him. "You're thinking about it, aren't you? About having your own little spread somewhere and raising a family. I think about it too, a little differently, but the same idea—the old nesting instinct."

"Yeah, something like that." He lifted her face and kissed her lightly on the lips, twice. "Now, pretty lady with ink on her nose, are we going to print a newspaper or aren't we?"

They printed. Three hundred strokes of the counter-weight four times. When they were done, Morgan's arms felt the strain.

"Sure we need three hundred?" Morgan asked.

"I promised my advertisers that I print three hundred, so I'm going to print three hundred. If fifty of them don't get read, it isn't my fault."

It had taken them a half hour to print each page. Then they began collating and folding them.

"Seems like I did this last week."

"Sure it's been a week? I'm not so sure, maybe we printed it early."

They didn't distribute the papers that night. Instead they locked the doors and went up to her apartment. They had coffee and talked. She told him about her childhood and her newspapering father and he talked a lot about the Spade Bit.

"You want it back, don't you? You want to raise horses again over there in Idaho."

"Yes. But that's impossible until I rob a good sized bank. Yes, I've thought of it more than once. The problem is you have to get enough money, and get away clean, not get killed in the process or let anyone know who you are. Bounty hunters can be murder."

They went to bed early, just like an old married couple and she rolled toward him and kissed him hungrily. They made love softly, gently, and then both fell asleep.

Morgan woke up a little after midnight. A bell clanged furiously somewhere outside.

Charlie woke and sat up beside him. She shivered. He put his arm around her.

"What is it?"

"Fire bell. I better check to see that this place isn't on fire."

She ran down the steps naked. Morgan pulled on his pants, then his boots and followed.

She stood at the front door peeking out from the blind.

"We're not on fire. But I can see it down the street."

"I'll go check it out. Morgan hurried back up the stairs, grabbed a shirt and his gun belt and strapped it in place, then ran back down.

Outside he could see the blaze at once. It was in a small store standing alone at the end of the second block fifty yards from the nearest neighbor. It was on the Merriweather side of the street and had been a small store that catered to woman who liked to have dresses made to order.

The fire was well along. A small pumper charged up behind one horse and three men cranking the handles to build up pressure in the water tank. But only a feeble stream of water came from the two inch hose.

Nothing could save the building. The tanker moved down the street and wet down the cedar shingle roofs on three businesses, then did the same on the other side.

More than a hundred people gathered to watch the fire.

"See everybody at a fire," one older man said as he leaned on his cane. "Ain't missed one now in forty years, man and boy, no matter where I lived."

"You start it on fire," Morgan asked.

"Sure as hell not! I just watch 'em, don't start them."

The fire burned hotly for another twenty minutes. The dry pine lumber made good fuel and bolts of cloth and laces and other stitchery goods in the building added to the heat. By the time the roof fell in, half the spectators vanished, and soon there were only a few men around.

"Volunteer firemen," somebody said pointing to the men. "They don't do much good usually, but they think they do."

Lee walked over near the fire and saw two of the firemen at what had been the rear corner of the building. They seemed to be sniffing the air.

Morgan walked up beside them and sniffed as well.

"You're right," he told them. "That's coal oil. Either the ladies used a lot of lamps or somebody doused the back of this building good with coal oil before they set it on fire. No wonder you couldn't stop it."

The firemen looked at him and scowled. "Damn! Think you're right," one of them said.

Morgan headed back toward the newspaper office. He wondered why somebody would burn down a dressmaker's shop. He snorted. The only reason he could come up with was that the fire had some connection with the Town Meeting. Could have. He was about to go into the newspaper office when he heard a shout up the street. Two blocks ahead he could see a new fire glowing in the night sky.

Lee ran that way and by the time he was a block closer he could tell the fire was on the other side—the Wert side—of the street. It was a building about the same size, and from the striped pole outside, Morgan figured it was a barber shop. This fire didn't have the start the first one had. But the tanker fire truck was empty.

Lee joined in a bucket brigade and they managed to put out about half of the fire, but the part in back burned brightly through the buckets of water. Lee moved in close enough and sniffed.

"Coal oil," he said softly, then returned to the bucket line.

It was tit for tat, almost. This building would have to be torn down even though they saved about half of it. The roof was still up, but tottering.

Lee went back to the newspaper office. He told Charlie about the two stores, and how he smelled coal oil on each one.

"Those two old men going to burn down the town just to spite each other?" Charlie asked.

"Let's hope not," Lee said. "Where would you get any advertising for the *Observer*?"

They went up the steps to the bedroom and Lee lit a match to see what time it was. Two-thirty.

They settled back in bed and Charlie pressed close to him until they fit front to back like a pair of spoons.

"Love to do this," Charlie said and yawned.

"Sexy," Morgan said.

"Mmmmmmm," Charlie got out before she dropped off to sleep.

"Damn sexy," Lee said and grinned. Hell, it was almost like they were married.

Neither one woke up until morning.

Morgan came awake late, almost a quarter to seven. The first thing he realized was he was in Charlie's bedroom and he could smell coffee boiling and fried potatoes, cheese and onions cooking in the kitchen. He was up and dressed and hurried into the cookery.

Four eggs sunnyside up, a skillet full of fried potatoes and cheese and onions, three slices of toast and jam and three cups of coffee later, Morgan was ready for business.

"That's the big trouble not having any gainful employment," Lee said. "How in hell can you know when you're through and can loaf around?"

Charlie took a swipe at him. "You can help me deliver the *Observer*."

"Afraid I did that once. Any more and you would start *expecting* me to help, and we'd have a fight, and I wouldn't get to tweak your nipples any more."

"Try right now if you want to," she said. Her face was in that vulnerable, open, ready expression. Then she grinned. "Or later if you don't have time now. That was beautiful last night, just laying there close and feeling safe and protected and . . . and loved. It was just wonderful."

"Way it always should be," Morgan stood and stretched. "But I've got to see a man today. Got to talk to old Gramps Merriweather and remind him not to hire anyone to blow his brains out for two weeks. He promised me."

"If he breaks his promise to you, there won't be much left for you to do about it."

"True, so I'll touch base with him. Does this town have a baseball team?"

"Baseball team? I don't think so—this year. First year I was here there were three teams that played each other. They tried to get four, but the fourth one never quite made it. You play?"

"Some."

She looked at him. "Meaning you're probably damn good. What position?"

"You know about baseball?"

"I'm the sports reporter here, too." They both laughed.

He waved at her and walked down the steps and out the back door to the alley. Wasn't a good idea to advertise sleeping over with the newspaper lady.

A few minutes later, Morgan stood looking at the display of hats in the store window. Might be nice. Naw, didn't need one. His dad used to say, *don't fix it if it ain't broke.* He also said, *don't throw it away if it ain't worn out.*

He was ready to move when someone came up beside him. A woman. He looked over.

"Well, the heiress, Miss Merriweather."

"Good morning. You sneaked out on me the other day."

"Best that way, sometimes."

"Not with me. We need to talk business. I want you to help Gramps convince the locals to push for the town route for the railroad."

"They already voted that way yesterday."

"Sure, and last night Wert burned down one of Gramp's stores."

"Then one of Wert's stores was torched," Lee said. "Both of them stunk of coal oil. No accident, either one."

"That's what I mean. Wert will do anything to run that railroad down the Wallowas."

"You can't stop an idea with a bullet."

"A bullet would stop Wert. No, no, I really don't mean that. It just popped out. What in the world can we do?"

"Sit tight. I'd say your team is ahead about

four to zero going into the last of the ninth inning. Don't do anything stupid, dumb or risky and you should win the game."

"This isn't a baseball game! If that railroad goes the other way, La Grande could shrivel up right here and die."

"Probably not, but damn sure it wouldn't grow like it could with the road coming through. You seen those railroad men yet?"

"No, I was looking for them." She blushed. "I thought . . . I thought I might have them up to the house for supper . . . or something."

Morgan chuckled. "They'd probably like the 'or something' better. Depending on the men. Of course, it could come under the something stupid category, too."

"Well, you let me worry about that. I'll take care of it. Oh, somebody is looking for you. A man named Alonzo Baer. He's not a nice man at all."

"He work for Wert?"

"Yes."

"Figures. I'll go see Wert, he probably wants to find out if I burned down his business last night."

"Did you?"

"No. Counterproductive."

"What?"

"Big word that means it would bring about the opposite results I want."

"That's not the only big thing about you. Why don't you come see me tonight. Use the alley door."

"I'll check. I may have some man-type things to do. Never can tell. Don't hold supper for me."

Morgan turned and walked the other way. He

had heard of Alonzo Baer. The man was said to be something of a local celebrity as a fast gun, and was not at all bashful about proving it to anybody who would draw. Might have to find out some day just how fast this Baer really was.

Morgan walked toward the bank. Town this size should have more than one brick building, Morgan decided as he pushed open the big door to the money place and went inside.

Chapter Nine

This time the president's door was closed at the Wert Home Bank of La Grande. Morgan started toward the barrier but the young man at the nearby desk looked up.

"Mr. Wert is busy, sir. Could I help you?"

"No, I need to see Wert. Tell him Lee Morgan is here."

"I'll need to wait a few minutes. He told me that this was an important meeting."

"Good, you sit there and wait," Morgan said.

He took four long strides to the door, turned the handle and walked inside while the lackey called out something behind him.

Wert was in an important meeting. A well used redhead with her dress top around her waist sat on his lap and Wert had one of her breasts in his mouth. His pants were open and his limp tool lay there between the redhead's bare legs.

"What in hell?" Wert sputtered dropping the

fleshy morsel.

"Don't let me interfere with a serious meeting like this," Morgan said. "You just go right ahead with whatever important matter you were considering. I won't take but a minute. I hear you want to see me, Wert. Go right ahead with your business there. I know how hard it is for a man of seventy-five to get a hard-on. Just keep working on him, girl. He'll get it firmed up eventually."

Lee had closed the door behind him and now he flipped the night lock on the door.

He turned back to Wert who had sat up abandoning the big breast and its brown nipple.

"Damnit, Morgan! What the hell you mean busting in here like this and—"

"And what the hell do you mean starting to burn down the goddamn town? You hired somebody to torch that dress shop last night with coal oil. You think Merriweather was going to knuckle under and let you get away with it?"

Wert pushed the whore off his lap and pointed to the back door. She pulled up her dress, then held out her hand and Wert gave her three dollars.

Morgan shook his head. "Wert, I figured you could afford a better whore than the three dollar kind. Get one next time that isn't used up, worn out and has lost all of her sparkle. Now, what did you want to see me about?"

"You son of a bitch!" Wert said.

The woman waved at them both, grinned at Morgan, and went out the side door into the alley.

"Next time you open your fly, lock your door. Now, old man, did you want to see me or not?"

Wert buttoned his fly and pushed his shirt into

his trousers. When he felt a little more put together, he glowered at Morgan.

"I should kill you!"

"But you won't because you need me. Hell, so you have trouble getting it up sometimes. I've had the same trouble. Yeah, at my age. Happens now and then. Forget it. You got a job for me?"

"Thinking about one. Just stay away from that Merriweather clan. They're poison. You see the railroad men today?"

"Nope. Must have got delayed."

"Get out of here, Morgan. Come back tomorrow. And knock, goddamnit!"

Morgan grinned as he left the room. Nothing to keep the boss on his toes like barging in on him.

Lee marched down the street until he found a saloon open and walked inside.

Alonzo Baer seemed to be holding an impromptu question and answer session with a man who already had a bloody nose and one eye half closed.

"Then you admit you set the barbershop on fire?" Baer demanded.

"Hell, no. Didn't do no such thing."

The speaker was slightly smaller than Baer, heavy but with little muscle. He wiped blood off his nose and looked at his hand, then cleaned it on his blue shirt.

"You admit that you bought two gallons of coal oil from the hardware store yesterday afternoon."

"Yeah, everybody buys oil for their lamps."

"Two gallons at once? A gallon will do the average house for six months. Why you need a whole year's supply? And when we checked at your place we found only one old rusty tin half full. Not the bright shiny tins Herkimer sells now. What did you do with the two gallons, Pailey?"

"Must have lost them."

Alonzo hit him a short, stiff right fist to his nose that splattered the already mashed flesh even more. Pailey jolted backwards, hit the bar with his shoulders and skidded down to the floor.

"Get up, Pailey. We gonna have a long talk. You don't give the right answers, you get hit again."

Pailey stood slowly, lifted his hands in a futile gesture, then slashed his foot upward at Alonzo's crotch. Alonzo tried to jump backwards, but didn't quite make it. His .44 cleared leather just as the boot hit his crotch and he bellowed in agony as his testicles smashed into pulp. He dropped to the floor screaming, his eyes tightly closed and his body curled into a protective ball.

Pailey paused a moment to look at Alonzo Baer, a gloating expression wreathed his face. Baer still held the six-gun. He bellowed as he opened his eyes, lifted the Colt and sent three shots into Pailey's chest as fast as he could cock the weapon.

Pailey went down holding his blood stained shirt front, a look of surprise and disbelief on his face. Then he tumbled forward and lay on his stomach on the rough wood floor. He didn't move.

The barkeep went around and leaned over Pailey.

"He's dead, Alonzo. What the hell we gonna do now?"

"Get a six-gun and put it in his damned hand. Now!"

The apron hurried behind the bar for the

protection six-gun he kept there.

Baer still had tears in his eyes from the gushing pain in his scrotum. At last he could sit up with only a small cry of pain. He stared around the saloon. There were only three other men there, one drunk at a nearby table could have no idea what happened. He had passed out where he sat ten minutes ago. A young cowboy had been nursing a beer at the stand up bar.

He held up his hands. "Hey, I didn't see a damn thing. I been drinking a half hour or so and turned to go to the outhouse. Then I heard the shots and when I looked back, the guy was dead. If you say he had a gun, he had a gun."

Baer looked at Morgan.

"Yeah, I know you, Lee Morgan. Mr. Wert said I should talk to you. You saw Pailey pull his gun after he nut kicked me, right?"

"Sounds right to me," Morgan said. "No money out of my pocket one way or the other."

"Keep our story that way," Alonzo said. He looked back at the barkeep who had just pushed an unfired six-gun under the dead man's side.

"Go get the sheriff, barkeep. Let's get this over so I can go see Doc Stanton. My damn balls are killing me!"

Morgan waited until the sheriff came. His name was Higgins, Jim Higgins, and he was about what Lee expected. An older man who didn't wear a gun and had a deputy with him who was young and carried a six-gun and a shotgun.

The questions were quick and brief. Sheriff Higgins asked Baer what happened. The cowboy confirmed it and Morgan nodded. Three sober witnesses agreed that it had indeed been a matter of self defense and Pailey had drawn first.

Lee finished his beer and went outside. A dozen people were grouped around, trying to find out what had happened. A second deputy with a shotgun kept them outside the bar until the sheriff was done.

Charlie ran up. "Heard there was a shooting?"

"Yep."

"So tell me about it. What happened? Were you there, inside? Did you see it?"

He told her Alonzo's version of the story. "You can get the same thing from the Sheriff's report."

"Sure, but an eye witness is better." She paused. "Is that what really happened? Alonzo Baer is known around here for being a bit quick to use his weapon."

"For right now, that's what happened," Morgan said.

"You might tell me what really took place later?"

"Might. Depends."

"What were they arguing about?"

"Just leave it alone, Charlie. Whatever we say won't bring back the dead man and won't convict the killer. Leave it lay."

"Sure. This is the third man Alonzo has killed this year. All of them were self-defense. He works for Wert, you know. Whatever dirty work Wert can't stand to do himself, he has Alonzo do. Like foreclosing on widows, and booting grandmothers into the street in the middle of winter. That might apply to murder, too. If so, I want to know. Alonzo is not our most upstanding citizen."

"Figures. I got a call to make."

"Mr. Merriweather?"

"Yep. Want to be sure he keeps his promise to

me not to get himself killed."

They nodded. Lee said he would see her later and went through the Grande Ronde General store to the alley and down to the Shotgun Saloon's back door. Inside he asked the barkeep if the old man was in.

"Yes, with a lawyer."

"Good, I've been wanting to talk to him, too."

Before Tupot could object, Morgan walked behind the bar and down to the door. He knocked once and pushed the panel open. Rudolph Merriweather glanced up with a frown that soon turned into a smile.

"Yes, Morgan. Glad you're here. I'm rewriting my will. Oh, this is John Calder, my lawyer." The legal man was thin, graying into his fifties with spectacles and a nervous tick over his right eye. He held out his hand and Morgan took the limp handshake.

"I'm making damn sure that Franny gets at least 51 percent of my entire holdings. John says if I do that, she'll have almost no chance under Oregon law of contesting the will with success. No, no, I'm not planning on dying anytime soon, but I want it set up right."

"Good. That promise we made still holds?"

"For the two weeks? Of course. Always been a man of my word."

"How about extending it to 15 years?"

Merriweather grinned. "Yeah, might do that. Be nice to touch the century mark. Might just be damn good at that. Hell, why not? First though, I need to set Franny up in some kind of business or service or job to keep her busy. Otherwise I'm afraid she's going to get pregnant, and I won't stand for being no great grandpa."

Morgan thought for a minute. "Put her in charge of all of your real estate. Let her collect the rents and see to the repairs of any new building. She's bright, educated. I think she'd be good at it. Also, be nice for you two to be speaking again."

He sighed, thinking about it. "Yeah, yeah, might work. She couldn't do much damage that way. John, draw us up a contract between Franny and me. Give her some of the work you've been doing on the properties, and give her a salary, say a hundred a week, and she reports to me. She can't buy or sell property without my approval . . . you know the usual safeguards."

"Be pleased to do that, Rudolph. Take a couple of days."

"Fine, fine."

"Oh, one more thing," Morgan said. "You know a man named Pailey?"

Merriweather looked up quickly and nodded.

"Alonzo Baer just killed him in a brawl in a saloon. Sheriff said it was self defense. Though you would want to know."

"Goddamn! Something should be done about that Baer. That's the third man he's killed that I know of. All self-defense. Bet Pailey didn't have a gun. He never wore one. No hideout either. Didn't like guns, he told me once. Damn! John, see that his widow gets . . . three hundred dollars from an anonymous donor."

"I'll do it today, Rudolph."

Morgan stood. "I better go. Remember that new agreement is for 15 years." Morgan held out his hand.

Merriweather smiled softly and shook the big paw. "You bet. I'm thinking more positively now.

Yes, 15 years and the railroad right through the edge of La Grande!"

Morgan went outside through the alley door and looked at the bright sun. It was a great day to be alive, unless your name was Pailey.

He walked down to the General Store's rear entrance and went inside. He couldn't think of a thing he needed to buy so he continued on to the street.

Morgan walked a half block when he heard a woman scream. She had just come out of a store with a package in her arms when she shrieked and dropped the goods and rushed back inside.

Lee saw the cause of her fright. Facing the merchant's door stood Kid Texas. He had been pointing his .32 caliber revolver at the woman and chuckled as she rushed back inside the store. He lifted the gun and blew across the muzzle, then pushed it back into the holster and turned and walked up the street away from Morgan.

Lee saw an eldery gentleman using a cane walking toward the kid. When the old man was ten feet from Kid Texas, the youngster called out sharply.

"You there with the cane. Drop it and raise your hands or I'm gonna draw on you and shoot you down like a dog!"

The old man stared at the youth for a minute, then snorted and walked ahead.

Kid Texas drew, and for a moment, Morgan forgot he was a kid of fourteen. His draw was smooth, much practiced and he heard the hammer click back into the cocked position.

The kid lifted the weapon as he was cocking it, his point and shoot system worked and the gun centered its aim on the old man's chest.

"Don't move or you're dead!" Kid Texas barked. The old man had stopped when he saw the real gun and heard the hammer lock back. He frowned for a moment, then he rushed forward, his cane flailing the air.

Kid Texas wasn't sure what to do. He hesitated a moment too long and the elderly man was on him. The cane hit Kid Texas' wrist and beat the arm downward. The cane came down again and once more, slamming painfully into the youth's shoulders.

Then the gray haired man caught hold of his temper. He pushed Kid Texas down to the boardwalk and laid the cane on his shoulder.

"Henry, I told you never to do that again. Somebody could of seen you and hurt you bad thinking you was really going to shoot. I'm going to tell your ma, and she'll be damn mad about this."

He took the gun from the Kid's hand. "You git home and you tell your ma, and when you come to my house and apologize, I just might give you back your deadly toy gun."

Kid Texas nodded but didn't say a word. He jumped up and ran down the street. The old man hooked up the gun, pushed the barrel behind his belt and walked on down the street, the cane seemingly not so necessary now.

Morgan hoped that Henry, Kid Texas, had learned a lesson from his run-in with an obvious friend of the family. Pulling a stunt like that on a stranger could get the kid killed.

Chapter Ten

"Lee Morgan, I've been looking all over town for you."

Morgan recognized the voice before he turned and found Franny Merriweather standing just behind him on Main Street's boardwalk.

"We need to talk, Morgan. My house in half an hour. You be good you can stay for supper, or dinner as they say in Chicago. Come to the alley door. I have a problem you can help me with."

"A real one?"

"I'm afraid so. It has to do with our good friend, Mr. Merriweather."

She turned and went the other way. It was a brief encounter, but four stores down the street, Alonzo Baer saw the exchange.

Now what the hell are they talking about, he asked himself. He decided to follow Morgan. It wouldn't be hard. That hat with the red diamonds on it stood out like a beacon. The fact that Morgan was half a head taller than most of the other people on the La Grande street helped as well.

Baer held back watching Morgan. He loafed along Main Street, he went into a small meat market and grocery store and came out with an apple which he promptly bit into. He looked like a man in no rush.

Morgan ambled down the boardwalk, but when Baer looked for him again, he had vanished. The alley. Alonzo hurried up to the alley and looked around. He saw someone he figured was Morgan turning the corner into the next street. He went west, toward the big Merriweather mansion where the girl lived.

Yeah, highly likely. Alonzo ran down the alley and looked around the wooden building into First Street. There he was, walking faster now down First. Still heading for the girl's place. She lived there alone, except for a stay-over cook.

Baer kept out of sight moving from cover to cover, but at no time did Morgan check his back trail. He was either on an innocent walk or the man had nerves of steel. Wert had been specific. He didn't want Morgan talking to the Merriweathers. Now here he was heading for the girl's house.

Two blocks later, Baer saw Morgan turn into the alley behind the Merriweather house. He got to the end of the alley just as someone let Morgan in through the back door off the alley of the Merriweather place.

Yes! Had him. Now maybe Wert would listen to reason.

Ten minutes later Slocum Wert scowled as he

listened to what Alonzo told him.

"You certain they talked in the street, then parted and Morgan took a round-about way to her house?"

"Absolutely. I stayed well back. He went to her place after wasting some time along Main Street. I'd bet that he's in there now with her. Let me take him out, Mr. Wert. Morgan is a man who won't back down from a gunfight."

"One killing a day is enough. I told you just to scare Pailey, not murder him. You were lucky on that one. Damn lucky. No, I can't permit another gunfight."

"I could bushwhack him with a rifle when he goes into the hotel tonight," Baer suggested.

"No, not in town. We'll think of something. If he's working with them, he has to be eliminated." Wert paced back and forth behind his desk. At last he grinned.

"Yes. A test. We'll tell him that the girl is influencing her grandfather and that can upset our campaign with the railroad to put the line in where we want it. The girl has to die in an accident. A buggy accident."

"She seldom drives a buggy," Alonzo said. "Many a time I've wished I could catch her alone in a buggy and rip those fancy clothes off her and shove mine into her about three times."

"Enough of that, Baer. Get back out there and watch her house. See if he comes out this afternoon or tonight. Stay there all night if you have to."

"Yes sir."

"Just be sure that you don't *accidentally* shoot him before we figure out what to do. If you see him away from her house, like on Main Street, tell him I want to see him tomorrow at nine. You be here, too. By then I'll have a good plan worked up to take out both of them, for good."

Morgan slipped in the back door of the Merriweather mansion and saw the cook. She was a slender Chinese girl who bowed twice but said nothing as she led him into the living room.

"Lee, I know it was a chance talking to you on the street, but I wanted to risk it. I talked to Mr. Calder today. Evidently he had good news for me. He said Grandpa wants me to take over the real estate part of his business, manage the rentals and any new buildings and the mortgages he holds. Isn't that exciting! I had some economics in school at Eugene, but I'm not sure I can do all of this."

"Not sure?" Morgan laughed. "Franny, you're a natural at managing things. You have the education, you can learn about interest rates and repairs and all of that quickly. I'm sure that this lawyer will help you. I met him this afternoon at your grandfather's office."

"I'm supposed to talk to grand dad tonight at supper at the Delmonico's restaurant." She paused and looked at him. "You really think it's a good idea?"

"Best thing that's happened to you since you met me," Morgan said. She had taken off the little jacket that went with the soft summer frock. Slender straps went over the shoulders and a square cut neckline gave a dark promise of cleavage.

"I like that dress," Lee said. "It shows just enough of you to drive a man crazy."

"With desire?" she asked, smiling. "Yes, I'll go

have supper with Grandpa. I guess it's time that I eased up on him. He is back to normal. Trouble was, I never liked him too much when he was himself."

"That's because he was your combined parents. He was authority, the boss. Not unusual. I'd probably react the same way. Now you're grown up, you can see things with a lot more clarity."

"Yeah." She grinned and rubbed her breasts through the thin fabric. "You have a couple of spare minutes."

They had been standing just back of the windows, looking out at the town and the mountains beyond. Now he went to her and held her shoulders and kissed her lips tenderly. Then his arms went around her and his lips burned into hers. When their lips parted he pushed her back and opened his fly.

His penis sprang out, hard and ready for action.

"Can you play the flute?" he asked.

"With the best you've ever had," she said. She dropped to her knees and sucked him into her mouth. For a moment he was afraid she would never stop taking it in. It must have gone halfway down her throat. Then she let him out aways and began pumping back and forth with her head.

"My god, Franny, you must have also taken a course in music to learn how to play so well. You already got me worked up halfway to exploding."

She laughed as best she could with her mouth full and continued.

Morgan looked up and saw the Chinese girl coming into the room. She had a tray with a bottle and glasses and a plate of fruit. She put the tray down on the table near the two and looked at her mistress.

Franny let go of him for a minute and looked at Ming.

"Be a good girl, Ming, and help me entertain Mr. Morgan." At once Franny went back, accepted his penis in her mouth, and began pumping in and out of him.

Morgan had been startled by the entrance of the girl, now he looked on in wonder as the slender girl worked a sash and slipped out of the one piece garment she wore. She stood naked before him and he was surprised at how large her breasts seemed on her slender frame. She came up to him, caught his hands and put them over her breasts.

She smiled. "I like," she said. She let him fondle her mounds, bringing them to a soft glow of warmth, and her nipples rose and filled with warm blood.

Then she pulled away and brought over a chair so she could stand on it. Morgan still stood on the floor with Franny on her knees at his crotch.

Ming stood on the chair and was just right to push one breast into Morgan's mouth. She took his hands and put one at her muff of soft black hair and the other one in back against her round little ass.

"Finger me," she said.

Morgan tried to laugh, but his mouth was filled with tit. He pushed his fingers downward, found her node and twanged it twice, then moved down to her slot. It was wet and ready. He pushed one, then two fingers into her and began to pump.

"Yes, yes!" she cooed. Then she took his other hand and pushed it toward her other hole. The small girl began to climax. That brought on Morgan's own surge and he pumped hard into the hot mouth beside him and grunted and moaned as he loosed his load.

At the same instant he felt Franny's arms wrap around his legs as she slammed into a climax of her own moaning and shaking and spasming her way to fulfillment.

They all came down about the same time and slumped to the floor, still entwined and penetrated. They lay on the soft carpet on the living room floor panting and gasping for breath.

As he edged back toward normal, Morgan pulled the girls up beside him and lay with his arms around each of them.

"Now that is what I call a first," he said. "Nothing like that ever before."

"And probably never again. Ming and I never repeat ourselves. We work up new and different entertainments."

"Ming was a surprise."

"That's how to keep a man interested, keep surprising him. It always works."

Ming touched his face and he looked at her slightly slanted eyes and her flat nose. She smiled. "You poke Ming now?"

Morgan chuckled. "Not for a few minutes. I have to rest up."

"Ming next," she said softly.

Morgan looked at Franny.

"What's the matter, you don't like Chinese?" Franny asked laughing.

"It's all right with you?"

"Of course. Ming and I share in lots of things. If neither of us have a man for a while, we share each other. But not tonight. That would be a waste."

They all three rested.

Morgan lifted up on one elbow and looked at Franny. "Hey, I just had a thought. I mean, if you wouldn't mind, maybe I could come over some night and . . . sort of . . . you know. Watch the two of you sharing each other."

They both hit him and tickled him and chased him around the room. They collapsed on a couch laughing.

"It was just an idea," Morgan said. "It would be another first for all of us."

"Forget it," Franny said. "As I remember, you have an appointment with Ming."

Ming squealed and rolled on top of Morgan and the two girls stripped his clothes off.

It was past six that evening when Morgan managed to slip away from the big mansion owned by the Merriweathers. He felt a little overworked, but what a wonderful feeling.

Morgan took a note from the room clerk and collapsed on his bed without reading the message. He got up about ten o'clock and undressed, lit a lamp and read the note. It was in a sealed envelope.

"Morgan. Meet me at my office at 9 A.M. tomorrow. Don't be late." It was sighed with a scrawl that he at last made out to be Wert.

Lee looked at the note again, put it on the dresser and dove into the bed. He slept without waking until six A.M. He washed his face and body to the waist, put on a new blue shirt and some blue jeans and a fancy buckskin fringed vest he had found in the general store.

After breakfast, Lee walked the town. He was starting to see some differences between the two sides of the street. The Merriweather side had better looking buildings, they were painted, kept in repair and had good shingle roofs. The other side of the street, with the exception of the bank, had buildings not as well made, and with little or no upkeep. Strange now that he thought of it. He'd ask old man Merriweather.

At 8:55 A.M. Morgan banged on the front door of the bank. The skinny, Fancy Dan from the front desk lifted the shade and looked at him, frowned and unlocked the door.

"This is a stick up!" Morgan whispered to the man and pushed his finger in his ribs. The young man lifted his hands, his face went starkly white and he almost fainted.

"Yeah, I feel safe with you here protecting my money. I've got an appointment with the boss at nine."

The ex-bank teller who had risen to be first assistant to the vice president couldn't speak. He wiped sweat off his forehead with his hand and pointed at the President's open door. Slowly the color came back to the young man's face, and Morgan snorted in derision as he walked away from the milktoast man.

A short time later, Morgan looked up and swore softly. "What the hell did you just say?" he asked Wert.

"I said the girl is the dangerous one. The old man is almost dead anyway. She'll inherit most of it and that is my problem. I want you to take the girl for a buggy ride up Catherine Creek on a nice little picnic, crash the buggy, and sweet little Fran Merriweather will be tragically killed."

"I told you a week ago I don't do hired killings. No. Absolutely not. That was a condition of my employment. Let your top gunman, Baer, do it. He likes to kill. I watched his eyes as he cut down that guy in the saloon."

"Then you're refusing an order?"

"Hell, no. You can't give me that order because you agreed not to when I hired on. In my business we call those terms and conditions of employment. You agreed to them and you're stuck with them. You want to call it quits, that's fine with me."

"Now hold on! I paid for a month's service. I want my money's worth. So you'll do what I say."

"Not a chance. You ask any gun for hire. Conditions are laid down, accepted by both parties and the work done. No changes. Am I still working for you or not?"

"Hell, get out of here, I'll think about it."

Morgan went out of the bank by the back door the President used. He knew somebody was tailing him before he was halfway down the alley. He rounded a corner and waited for the man. The guy came around running, no gun out.

Morgan pounded the butt of his big Colt down on the man's head before he could see Morgan. The body tumbled into the dirt, out cold. Morgan rolled him over. Alonzo Baer, just as he had suspected.

Lee continued down the alley, jogging to put some distance between him and the Wert gunman. He got to the big Merriweather mansion before anyone was up. He knocked on the back door until Ming came and opened it.

She kissed his cheek, apologized for not being dressed and hurried up to her mistress's bedroom. Morgan followed her and marched into the room right behind Ming.

Franny sat up rubbing her eyes.

"Who is waking me up at such a ridiculous hour?" she shrilled. Then she saw Morgan.

"Something happened to Gramps?"

"No, to you. Slocum Wert just tried to hire me to kill you. You have twenty minutes to get dressed and pack a bag. You're moving out until this is settled."

"Moving, but I don't want—"

Morgan caught one arm and hoisted her out of bed. She slept naked when she was alone, too.

"No time to argue. Wert could put ten men after you and offer them five hundred dollars to the one who guns you down. You'd be dead within two days. Let's go now before somebody gets over here to watch all the doors."

They left thirty-five minutes later. Ming stayed in the house and would make it look as natural as possible. Lights would go on in the rooms as usual at night, including Franny's. Morgan carried the suitcase as they hurried down the alley, quickly across another street and down that alley. They came up the alley in back of the newspaper office.

The back door was open. Morgan pushed her inside and followed.

"Sit down right here and don't make a peep. I'll be back in a minute." He saw the lights on in the apartment and hurried up the steps.

"Sleep in late?" Morgan asked as he came into the kitchen.

Charlie had just finished washing dishes. She looked up and snorted, "Buster, I've been up since four A.M. trying to get the front page worked out. None of your smart talk."

"I've got a boarder for you. It's an emergency."

Quickly he told her about the danger to Franny.

"We've never been the best of friends."

"You don't know her. Besides, she might sink some money into this rag." He grinned telling her it was all right.

Charlie ran down the steps ahead of him, gave Franny a friendly hug and pointed up the steps.

"Our rooms are right up here, Franny. Now don't you worry about a thing. Nobody will know you're here and Morgan will get the problem taken care of before we know it. How about some breakfast? Bet you haven't had any yet? Eggs and bacon, or oatmeal? Coffee and a fresh peach straight off the stage?"

Morgan waved and moved down the stairway. He had some powerful jobs to do and he didn't even know where to start. One of the first ones was Alonzo Baer, and he had no idea where to find him.

Chapter Eleven

It was mid-morning when Morgan walked down Main Street. By now Alonzo must have reported back to Wert and they had made a deal to kill both Franny and one Lee Morgan. Others had tried.

He walked with his eyes in the back of his head. Everyone who moved rated a quick scrutiny. He avoided walking across alleys without checking them out. His back stayed mostly to the store walls. A rider moving fast down the street had his undivided attention.

So far no Alonzo. Morgan wished that he had hit the man harder on the head, or kicked him a dozen times and finished the job. He'd have to kill Alonzo sooner or later. Now Franny was at risk as well.

Ahead he saw a gunman's stance and Morgan froze. Only the man faced away from Morgan. Man? It was the boy, Kid Texas, and his hand was jerking iron from leather.

Morgan ran. But there was no sound of gunfire. A woman screamed and then Lee heard the crackling laugh from Kid Texas as he holstered his weapon and walked on forward.

The man in the buckskin vest relaxed for a moment. He had to get the boy off the street. Smash that .32 pop gun into a hundred pieces and slap him a dozen times. Morgan walked quicker after Kid Texas. Before he overtook him a booming voice came through the din of the morning street noises.

"Kid, you shouldn't tease the women that way pretending to be a gunman."

Morgan saw Alonzo standing in the street, his right hand near his holster. Kid Texas had stopped on the boardwalk and stared at the gunman thirty feet away.

"Boy, you want to draw down on somebody, try me. I'm here and waiting. You just walk out in the middle of the street so you don't kill nobody in the crowd."

Morgan ran forward, but he was too far away. Kid Texas snorted and stepped into the dust of the street and went to the center of it. He was no more than twenty feet from Alonzo.

"Now, big fast gun, you want to draw on somebody, try me. Got to learn your lesson. Young punk like you got to be taught damn good. Go ahead, you go for it first."

"No!" Morgan shouted. He was still a hundred feet away. Too far for even a lucky shot. He ran forward.

Kid Texas stood there in his gunfighting stance, legs spread a foot, hand at his right side, fingers twitching. He stared at the older man.

For a moment he almost cried. His face worked and he blinked twice, then his hand clawed for his weapon and it came up much faster than Alonzo figured it would.

He had not been ready. The .32 in the boy's hand fired first and then Alonzo's big .44 went off. But his aim was ruined when the .32 caliber slug ripped into his left shoulder spinning him slightly. If it had been a .44 it would have knocked him down. He gritted, screamed and fired all at the same time in a reflexive action.

The .44 round caught Kid Texas in the right forearm, halfway to his wrist. One of the bones broke as the round slanted off and went through and into the dirt. The boy jolted backwards, lost his balance and fell on the seat of his pants.

Morgan raced between the two and fired twice in the air.

"Enough!" he bellowed. Morgan glared at Alonzo. "Baer, what the hell's the matter with you, taking on a kid? Even at that he beat you clean. Put the iron away Alonzo, or die where you stand."

Slowly Baer pushed the weapon back in leather.

"Somebody go get Doc Stanton," a voice yelled.

"Hell, I don't need no doctor, just a scratch," Alonzo said, walking off.

A sheriff's deputy ran up, and Morgan indicated Kid Texas who sat on the ground holding his wounded arm. The deputy helped the boy up and walked him down the street toward the medical man's office.

Morgan had claimed the Kid's six gun. He opened it, pushed out the four remaining rounds and pocketed them. Then he went over to a heavy steel beam sticking out of a partly finished building, and methodically battered the revolver on the beam until the barrel broke off. He slammed the cylinder and the handle until the gun broke into a dozen pieces. He picked them up and threw the metal chunks into a trash barrel.

He was half a block farther along when Charlie caught up with him.

"You in the middle of another shooting I hear," she said.

"Yes, ma'am," Morgan said smiling.

Charlie was mad as hell about something and holding it in. She backed Morgan up against the saddle shop wall and took out a pad and pencil. Then she looked up at him with self control keeping her civil.

"Tell me all about it," she said. She looked around. Nobody was nearby so she stepped closer. "Franny is a beautiful girl, and nice. We're friends now. I also know that you've been ramming her."

Morgan laughed. "I'll never get used to your foul mouth. What makes you say that?"

"A woman can tell. I was sure, so I asked her, and she said she'd figured out the same thing about me. First we were both mad, but then we decided we can share. But I'm still mad. Didn't I take care of you well enough?"

"Damn right," he said softly. "You rammed my brains out. With Franny it was business. I was trying to find out about her Grandfather."

"Yeah, sure."

"I was, at first."

Charlie gave in slowly. She took a deep breath and stared at him, then grinned. "Hell, I guess I can share too. You just get this mess cleaned up in a rush so we can send Miss Moneybags back where she belongs."

A special coach rolled up the street. On the side it had a logo that said GREAT WESTERN RAIL-ROAD.

Morgan looked at it and pointed. "Now there is your top story. The railroad men just came to town."

"Right!" She kissed him on the cheek. "See you later!"

Charlie ran down the street and it was only then that Morgan realized that she was wearing a dress like an almost proper reporter lady.

Mason Rutledge looked out at La Grande with curiosity. The company had been subjected to more pressure to put the main line through here along two different routes than anywhere since it began on the Columbia.

He was anxious to see just what the big attraction was to this Eastern Oregon desertlike community. Lumber and business, he knew the components. That was about all. Rutledge was just fifty-five, and had taken to the easy life of a railroad field engineer with gusto after many years in the main eastern office.

He loved the good life, a fine cigar and a great dinner. He also liked to see new places and new faces. He rode alone in the carriage. The driver was topside. They pulled to a stop at the Wert Hotel where he had mailed his intentions and shortly was shown to the hotel's Presidential Suite. There were three rooms on the top floor. Two beds, a sitting room and a large parlor for entertaining.

"Yes, this will be fine. I've had a long trip and I

POWDER CHARGE • 121

want to rest up before supper. I'll begin talking to people sometime tomorrow, if anyone asks."

He spoke to the manager of the hotel, a nervous little man with black hair combed forward to cover up his bald spot. He wore a suit and tie and was properly respectful of this important man just the way Mr. Wert had ordered him to be.

Rutledge tried the bed and smiled. A feather-bed! You didn't see many of them in commercial hotels. He had just slipped his shoes off when someone knocked on the door.

He went to the door and opened it. A young woman walked past him into the room and closed the door. She was attractive, well dressed and had just a touch of rouge. She smiled. "My name is Genevieve, and I was told to come here for some secretarial work. I hope that I'm not late."

"Secretarial work? I don't understand!" Rutledge watched her with interest but surprise. "I didn't order anyone to come to do secretarial work. There must be some mistake. Are you sure you have the right room?"

The girl grinned. "Mr. Rutledge, there are all sorts of secretaries. I'm more the social kind of secretary. The entertainment specialist who is here to see that you are comfortable, that you have a delicious dinner served in your room, and to do just *anything* that might help us bring you pleasure."

"Yes, you want my dinner order. Well, it's a little early and I had planned . . . ."

Rudolph stopped in mid sentence as the pretty girl began unbuttoning the fasteners down the front of her dress. The lower she went, the more sure he was that she had nothing on under the tight dress.

A moment later one breast popped out of her bodice. It was the biggest tit Mason had ever seen. A three-inch wide pure pink areola and pink nipple glowed at him. Then the twin breast swung out and Genevieve put her arms around Rutledge's neck and pushed her bareness up against his chest.

"You like my titties, Mr. Rutledge?" she asked.

He didn't have time to answer, because she eased back and pulled his face down on them. His mouth came open and she pushed it full of breast.

"Ohhhhhh my god!" he said, muffled around her soft pink flesh.

"You like that? Oh, good! I hope you like it. Ginny is here to do just . . . just any little old thing you want to do, Mr. Rutledge. You just chew away there for as long as you want to or move around some."

When Rutledge came up for air, she led him to the bed, sat down and pulled him on top of her as she lay backward. His mouth found her other breast and he growled as he chewed on it.

He eased back from her a minute later and realized that her legs were spread and he lay hard on her crotch. Goddamn!

"Let me lock the door!" he said softly.

She looked at him and smiled, reached up and kissed his lips. "Darlin' that's a good idea!"

Mason laughed softly. It was a test that never failed. She would do anything he wanted. She must be furnished with the compliments of the hotel. Anyway, he wasn't asking any questions. He locked the one outside door to the three

rooms and when he went back, Ginny had her
dress off and sat on the bed stark naked.

She had a curvy, delicious body like he had
never seen before. His wife was fat and never had
liked sex. Damn, but this one was something!

"Mason, why don't we get those old clothes off.
You look all hot and bothered with them on that
way."

She stripped him, kissing down each item,
leaving his short summer underwear for last,
then going into yelps and gasps of pleasure when
his stubby penis lifted up to the light.

"Oh, yes! Mason, we're going to have us one
fine lovin' party all night. I bet you're real strong,
probably good for five or six times!"

Mason sobered. He hadn't climaxed more than
once in 24 hours for so long he couldn't
remember when it had last happened. Five or
six? Hell, he could try!

Mason dove for the bed and pulled the willing
female over on top of him. "Right now, you on
top," he said and lifted her hips to move into the
right position.

"Just like riding a pony!" Ginny said showing
more enthusiasm than she had before. "I love it
this way."

An hour later Ginny was working him up again
when she stopped. "You aren't from the south,
are you?"

"South Boston originally, then Chicago."

"Good."

Ginny ran bare assed to the outside door and
knocked twice. There were three knocks in reply.
She unlocked the door and opened it, and a
small, slender, black girl walked in.

"Why you make me wait so long?" the girl

whispered.

"At least you were resting," Ginny whispered back. Then they both walked up to the bed.

"Mason, this is Ula."

Mason tried to pull the bedspread over his nakedness.

"Hey, no worry, she's with me, Mason. You ever had any black lovin'? You ever sucked on a black tit?"

Ula slipped out of her thin dress and stood before him black and sleek, slender and sexy, with big black breasts and a fine tight little bottom.

"Lord a'mighty!" Mason said. "This will be one great night to remember!"

He pulled Ula down beside him and kissed her breast, then chewed on her nipple before he sucked the mound half into his mouth. He came off her and laughed.

"Hell, the black don't come off! Ula, you taste the same way that Ginny does!"

They laughed and all three romped on the bed.

"Lordy, I never had me two women at once before, and I damn well never had any black ass!"

"Have mine!" Ula said and pushed her black bottom up to his face. Mason laughed and then went to work.

By midnight, Mason knew he would never make five, let alone six, but it was a goal worth trying for.

In his office in the back of the Gunsmoke Saloon, Rudolph P. Merriweather paced behind his desk. He stopped now and then and stared at the room clerk from the Wert Hotel who went off duty at 10 that evening.

"You say he came in about three this afternoon, went straight to his hotel room and hasn't come out since?"

"Yes sir. We took up a supper for two to his room. I'm sure there's one girl in there, and I think there might be two."

"Christ! Wert has thought of everything. Why didn't I know exactly when this man was coming?" He stopped. "No, not your fault. I should have been checking more careful. Figured the stage. Never thought of a private coach. Damn!"

He paced again. "You say he's in the suite on the top floor with two whores? And lights are still on?"

"Yes, Mr. Merriweather."

"You want to earn another dollar? Go find that druggist guy for me, the pharmacist. Have him get right over here. I'll make it worth his trouble."

A half hour later Douglas Ihander had what Merriweather wanted. He made up three small thin jars of the chemicals and stoppered them with corks.

Ihander put the bottles in Merriweather's hands and took the ten dollars.

"I don't want to know what this is for or how it's used. Then I can't tell anyone." Ihander turned and hurried out the alley entrance to the saloon.

Merriweather went outside and found young Harley. He had spotted him in the saloon earlier and told him he had a job for him. The eighteen year old was the pitcher on the town's only baseball team. He told Harley what he needed to do and the pitcher grinned.

"Hell, Mr. Merriweather, I can do all three of

them for sure. Big target like that."

Young Harley left with the three bottles and stood a minute across the street from the Wert Hotel. No throw at all, even on the third floor. Hell, he could hit the windows easy. Last three on the end. Damn, no problem at all. Young Harley took another snort from the flask in his pocket, then went halfway across the street and wound up.

The first bottle smashed through the window and splattered inside. The next two bottles did the same thing in the next two windows of the Presidential Suite.

Great Western Railway Company head route scout engineer, Mason Rutledge, yelled in surprise and fear when the bottles broke on the brass bed footboard. The smell was immediate.

"Rotten eggs!" Ginny wailed. The smell seemed to come from the smashed bottle and the fluid in it that splattered everywhere. Ginny wiped a spot off her leg and smelled it.

"Stink, stink, stink!" Ginny cried. She ran into the next room of the suite, and the next, and came back.

"All three rooms smell the same!" she screamed. "I'm getting out of here. How did this happen?"

She began pulling on her dress. Ula saw the shattered glass and stepped aroound it. "Just a little old stink bomb. Us kids down in Memphis used to get them all the time. They fun. Stink something wild, though." She slipped on her dress and the two women hurried into the hall and down the stairs.

Mason Rudolph sat on the bed. He was too exhausted to move. Hell, the smell would blow out of the room after a couple of hours. He went and opened the broken window wide, took a deep breath of the clean air and ignored the rotten egg smell the chemist had mixed up. Mason remembered the two girls and put the thought of a bad smell out of his mind as he crawled back into the soft bed.

Damn! What a night. Two whores in his bed and one of them just as black as the ace of spades. Rudolph chuckled. Evidently somebody wanted to give him some free floozy fun, but somebody else didn't want it to go so smoothly.

La Grande was gonna be one hell of a strange town to figure out where to run the railroad line. He turned over and almost at once went to sleep.

The rotten egg smell was still in the Presidential Suite the next morning when the girl came in to clean.

Chapter Twelve

That same night, Morgan spent some of his time dodging Alonzo. He saw the railroad man come into town, but he evidently went straight to a hotel room and planned on talking with the people the next day.

Morgan needed to get into the hotel to get his gear out. He decided his tab was no longer good there and Alonzo would have someone watching the place in case Morgan showed up again. But he wanted the new clothes, and his extra .45, and the other few things he traveled with that he hadn't lost.

He waited until eleven o'clock. Anyone watching the room would be getting tired by that time. He went in the side door off the side street and up the back stairs. Morgan took the steps softly at the far side so they wouldn't squeak. He could see down the hallway. A door down the hall from his on the opposite side of the corridor was open inward two inches.

A watcher.

Morgan pulled his hat down low, walked down the hallway as if half drunk, went past his door and kicked open the one that was cracked open. The Colt .45 in his hand came up and covered the man sitting in a straight backed chair watching out the door.

"What 'n hell?" the man crowed.

The Colt slammed down on top of his head, the side of the cylinder rapping him soundly. He pitched off the chair and lay on the floor unconscious.

Morgan pulled the door closed and went down to his room. He tried the door handle. Locked. The key from his pocket fit and he stood against the wall as he twisted the lock. He pushed the door inward with his boot.

At once a double-barreled shotgun roared and both loads of double-ought buck slammed through the thin door and past it where a man would be if entering the room.

Morgan squatted and looked around the door frame. A chair sat in the room six feet from the door. The shotgun had been tied to the chair, bound securely in place. A one-by-one inch stick had been used as a push rod to release both triggers when the door was forced inward.

No one was in the room. Morgan rushed inside, kicked the chair over, grabbed his new carpetbag and picked up some of his things scattered about. He stuffed them inside the bag and looked into the hall. Two men with shotguns came down the hall from the only steps.

Morgan reached around the door molding and fired two quick shots at the men who darted into open doors. Morgan than ran to the window, lifted it quietly, tossed his carpetbag onto the roof just outside the window and stepped out. He ran to the side of the roof and pushed off his carpetbag, then lowered himself until he held onto the roof by his hands and dropped the five feet to the ground.

By the time he was up and running with the carpetbag the shotgunners were at the window, but he was long out of range of their scatter guns.

He ran down the darkened side street to First, then on to the *Observer*. The lights were out. He tried the back door. It was unlocked. He slipped inside and laid the bar across the two steel holders locking the big door.

A light glowed up the stairway. A minute later a voice called. "Who's there?"

"Morgan."

"Good, you just about had buckshot for an early breakfast." The voice was Charlie's. "You coming up or staying down there?"

"I figure that bed is about full with two of you."

"Damn right, and I'm still mad."

"Tough turkey. I already got shot at once tonight, and I don't aim to challenge the stairway against a Greener."

"It's a Parker double-barrelled breach-loader but don't let that worry you. Worry that I know how to use it. Be a damn sight healthier for you to stay down there. I never did get to see that gent from Great Western Railroad. His name is Mason Rutledge and he's at Wert Hotel—probably with about three soiled doves if I know how Wert thinks."

"Probably."

There was a long silence.

"Yeah, I guess I just better find myself a sleeping place down here."

"Don't look too far. I threw down three blankets at the foot of the stairs." Charlie paused. "Morgan?"

"Yeah?"

"I'm still mad, but not too mad. And I can use this Parker, so you just behave yourself."

"Yes, ma'am. I seldom argue with a pretty woman holding a double-barrel ten gauge Parker."

"Good night."

"Yeah, maybe, we'll see."

The next morning Morgan woke up stiff and sore. He had spread out the blankets on some even boards down from the press and the morning light woke him. He had no idea what time it was. His Waterbury had stopped again.

He sat up and reached for his shirt and pulled on his boots. Upstairs he heard the women chattering. Morgan walked to the bottom of the stairs and called.

Charlie appeared quickly at the top of the steps with the Parker. "Oh, it's you. I figured it might be somebody looking for a handout, or maybe a burglar."

"You still mad?"

"No, but I don't know about Fran. Come up and ask her."

Morgan went up the steps warily. Sometimes you just couldn't tell about two women who got together this way, especially when you had been humping both of them.

He made it to the top of the stairs and walked

into the kitchen. Charlie turned around and smiled. She wore nothing above her waist. Her breasts bounced and jiggled.

"Good morning! How about some eggs and bacon for breakfast?" she asked, acting as if she were fully dressed.

Franny leaned out and turned, she too was bare to the waist. Her breasts were a little larger than Charlie's.

"The eggs are really good here, I've had two already. I can recommend them."

Morgan walked into the kitchen with a surprised expression that he couldn't get rid of.

"I still don't have my front page made up yet," Charlie said. "Suppose you'll have any time today to set a couple of stories for me? Fran offered but she doesn't know the type case."

"Also, I'm not a good speller. I just never tried to learn."

Fran was also acting as if nothing were out of the ordinary.

They made a place for him at the table, served him, chattered away about the paper and the railroad. And all the time not the slightest hint that they had their breasts hanging out. The only thing he could do was go along with it, pretend not to notice.

He ate breakfast, had coffee and then said he'd be back about noon to set the stories. Franny almost giggled once but held it in before Morgan could call her on it. He shrugged and headed for the stairs.

"You forgot something," Charlie said. "Don't I get a good morning kiss?"

She came toward him and pushed her bare breasts hard against him and she kissed him.

Then she stepped back quickly.

"Me too," Franny said. She held the kiss a little longer than Charlie had and her knee pressed to get between his legs. Then she slipped back from him.

"See you this noon," Charlie said and turned back to the kitchen. Franny waved and Morgan went down the steps and out the alley door. On an impulse he cut through the vacant lot beside the newspaper building and went to the street. He looked carefully down the street in both directions but could spot nobody watching the building. Then he saw something strange. The front door of the newspaper office had a knife stuck in it pinning a folded sheet of paper to the wood.

Morgan ran back into the newspaper rear door and told Charlie by shouting up the stairs.

"So get it and bring it in," Charlie said.

"Can't, I'm not even here. I don't want to get you in any trouble with Wert."

"Any more trouble, you mean," Charlie said.

She came down the steps wearing an ink stained blue shirt looking much more natural. She went past him and quickly to the front door, seemed surprised to see the note when she opened the panel. She pulled the knife out and took the note back inside.

She read it through before she gave it to him. "It's a trap," she said.

He took the note. It was written in block letters with a pencil by an unsteady hand.

"If you see Morgan, tell him he can make $500 with his gun if he meets me at the big bend of the Grande Ronde River at ten o'clock this morning. That's two miles upstream from town. Come alone. It's an easy $500."

"A trap," Charlie said. Suddenly she was holding him tightly. "Don't go," she said.

"I have to do. It's probably Alonzo Baer and one or two or three of his buddies with rifles. You have a rifle?"

She dug a Spencer carbine from a cupboard.

"I haven't fired it for a year."

She had a Blakeslee Quickloader with seven filled tubes of ammunition. Charlie looked again and found a box of 20 rounds of the .52 caliber ammunition.

Franny came down the stairs also normally dressed.

"What was it?"

"A trap to try to kill Morgan," Charlie said.

"Don't go," Franny said.

Morgan grinned. "This is the challenge of the job. They think they can kill me. It's man's greatest game, it's called life and death. If you don't win, it doesn't matter much."

The women looked at him and silently shook their heads.

"I need a horse but I can't go to the livery."

"Oh, damn! I have one in a little barn back there. But I still don't want you to go."

"This bend in the river. What's it like? Lots of trees, brush, open country?"

"Lots of trees along the river. The kids go swimming there because it's deep and a tree hangs out for a rope to swing on and drop in the water."

"Grampa never let me go out there," Franny said.

"I went every day I could the first year I was here," Charlie said.

"What time is it?" Morgan asked.

Franny looked at a small watch that hung around her neck on a gold chain. "Seven-thirty."

"Good, I'll be early. Hit the river and go upstream, right?"

They both nodded.

"Come show me your horse, I don't want to get shot as a horse thief."

Franny grabbed his arm, then kissed his lips. "You be careful out there."

"Damn right!"

He and Charlie ran out the back door. At the small open shed where the bay stomped, Morgan put on a blanket, then the saddle and cinched it up. He settled the old Spencer carbine in the boot and decided he was ready.

"Morgan."

He looked at her. "I really want you to come back. You let them kill you out here and I'll kick your corpse, I'll be so mad. You come back safe." She kissed him and her whole body helped pressing every inch of her against him.

He broke the kiss and swung up. "I'll be back, don't worry. Nobody's killed me yet."

Morgan rode away, slowly so he wouldn't attract any attention. Once he got out of town to the river, he turned upstream and rode hard. The first big bend was easy to find. He came at it from the north. He had ridden across the water at a low place and circled around two miles, so he could come in unobserved.

There was a small feeder stream where he tied up his horse when he was two hundred yards from the bend. He could see where there was a bare area that had been beaten down by horses and buggies. A baseball diamond had been laid out in the flat area nearby and two round fire rings had been built of loose rocks and stones.

Nobody seemed to be there. He watched closely. Bushwhackers could have come in last night just to be on the safe side. They could be sleeping yet, or alert with rifles waiting for him to ride in.

Morgan started using his outdoors expert knowledge. He watched for birds. A pair of crows sailed over the water and landed in a cottonwood that grew almost at the water's edge. They sat there a minute then took off cawing and cawing as they flew on upstream.

The hunter, Morgan, looked at the cottonwood, followed it down the crooked trunk and the two places it came from the ground. He scanned for movement. For a moment he saw nothing. Someone had to be there. The crows would not leave a favorite tree unless something scared them.

For a moment he thought he saw movement— an arm, a hand. He looked away, then back. Yes. Something was different. He concentrated between the two white and dark trunks. Morgan grinned. Yeah! He had one. The man had wedged himself into the crotch where the tree parted two feet off the ground. He had on a dark blue cap, a greenish shirt.

Morgan spotted the long gun. The man came for bear.

Now, with a point of reference he made some calculations. If he were setting up this ambush, he'd have a victim spot. Why not the rocks at the edge of the water about in the middle of the cleared area. It was just downstream from the actual bend, but a good viewing spot to watch the swimmers.

With that as the victim spot, and one man in the cottonwood, where would the best places be for a deadly crossfire for two more gunmen? He mentally cut the area into thirds. Two guns on one side and one on the other. The far side was widest. One more gun there. He found the perfect spot.

About thirty yards around the cleared area from the cottonwood lay a huge boulder, six feet high and twice that wide. It must have rolled down from some sudden upheaval millions of years ago. Now it was weathered and had brush growing around the near side. A man worming his way into the brush beside the rock would have perfect vision and a good field of fire. He could move quickly to solid cover to save his hide.

Yeah, that was a maybe. Now for this side. It was harder because he had no perspective. He cut the narrower area in half and checked for possibilities. A huge ponderosa pine towered over the area, stretching up eighty or ninety feet. It was four feet thick at the base and had been hit more than once by lightning.

Now there would be cover. It grew almost at the edge of the clearing. A little bit of judicious clearing and a man could have a good field of crossfire at the target.

Morgan began moving in that direction. He had trained with an Indian one summer. Over and over they had worked on tracking, on silent movement, on alertness in the woods. By the time the Sioux was ready to scalp Morgan, he had learned as much as he could.

He might never be mistaken for an Indian, but he got good enough so he could slip up on the Sioux teacher and make coup. Now he used that skill as he moved silently through the Eastern Oregon brush along the Grande Ronde River toward the big tree.

Morgan carried the carbine strapped across his back by the sling. He made sure his Peacemaker was firmly in his holster. Morgan moved in a crouched position to make a smaller target. He never put weight on his foot until he was sure that no branch would snap or no leaves rustle.

It took him ten minutes to move fifteen yards. By then he was in a slightly higher position where he could see the big tree. Morgan grinned. Ten yards ahead of him, two cowboy boots with legs attached extended toward him where a man lay beside the big ponderosa.

Now that he knew where he was going, Morgan moved quicker. He was behind the man, which helped. He checked the Colt, then the blade in his boot and moved again. A dozen feet the first minute. A third of the way. He crouched, pausing. The man lifted up. He saw a brown hat, a green and red checked shirt and an arm waving at someone across the way.

That was not good if the three could see each other. Morgan moved closer. At ten feet he pulled the knife from his boot. It was a new one with a five inch killing blade an inch wide, tapering to a point like a long slender triangle. Both sides of the knife were razor sharp all the way to the handle.

He put it between his teeth and crawled silently forward. He was four feet from the boots when the man came to his knees, looking out into the clearing. He grunted, whispered something and then flopped down on a soft bed of pine boughs he had cut for a cushion where he lay.

Morgan tried to breathe so quietly he couldn't hear himself.

A red winged blackbird sailed through the brush, then dipped toward the river.

Morgan crushed a young wild flower as he moved and wondered what kind it was.

Then he was just behind the man. He could reach out and touch his boots. He could see out of the man's tunnel of vision. He had cut away some brush and had a perfect field of fire around the big rocks.

Morgan checked but he could not see either of the other bushwhackers. There could be no mistake. There was no chance for mercy. The man lay in wait to kill someone, to kill Lee Morgan. Lee took the knife from between his teeth, raised up and dove forward. His left hand wrapped around the bushwhacker's throat cutting off any possible cry.

His right hand daggered down the knife, plunging it into the killer's back near his backbone, then slashing it sideways into the vertebrae. Three times he plunged the knife into the body before he surged forward, pulling away his left hand and slashed the man's throat with the knife.

The only sound was the soft sigh as the dead man's lungs emptied of their last breath of air. This time the kill did not provide the rush, the awe, that it usually did. It had been too easy. Morgan shivered slightly.

He wished he had a time piece. He searched the dead man's pockets and found a Waterbury. This one was from Sears, but that would do. The watch showed that the time was 9:45.

Morgan pulled back to the far side of the tree.

He had to find his own field of fire. Again he moved cautiously. Now was no time to make any noise or a mistake.

He edged closer to the clearing. A stump of a long cut pine tree showed to his left. On the far side of it he found what he wanted. A good view of the target rock and the other two suspected locations of the snipers.

He pulled back a little so they couldn't spot him, then he lay on his back so he could see an arc in back of him and rested. If the killers came on time, it shouldn't be long now before someone arrived.

Ten minutes later he rolled over gently. The sound of a horse galloping came through to him. He could see a quarter of a mile back toward town and there he spotted a lone rider on a pinto pony riding hard toward him.

When it happened, he would kill the pinto pony. Put a man on his feet in a fight and the man on a horse has a tremendous advantage.

The rider came closer. It looked like Alonzo Baer. Then Morgan was sure he was the man. He had the same dull gray hat with the sides rolled up.

Baer rode up to the rock, dismounted and ground tied the pinto. Then he looked around.

"Morgan!" he called. "Morgan, if you're hiding in the brush somewhere, it's time, ten o'clock. I can't make you any money until you come out here so we can talk."

Morgan had worked out the sequence long before. He had not had to figure it out, he simply knew. In a tough shootout you can't stop and figure out who or where to shoot next. If you did you were already dead. You simply had to know what to do. Lee knew.

He moved slightly so he could see the man in the low crotch of the cottonwood tree. He brought the Spencer around, made sure it had a full tube of rounds and one in the chamber. Then he sighted in on the man in the cottonwood. He was first. The horse second. Then Alonzo and a try at the man beside the big rock. He was the hardest one to be sure of.

Morgan took a deep breath and began to squeeze the trigger on the Spencer carbine.

Chapter Thirteen

Morgan fired. He saw the .52 caliber slug drill into the man's chest who sat in the crotch of the cottonwood tree. The puff of blue smoke from the round hazed the scene for a moment. He worked the lever and powered a fresh round into the Spencer repeater and cut down the Pinto with a head shot, then moved the muzzle toward Alonzo.

Gone.

He had dropped behind the rock. Morgan turned the weapon to the bushwhacker beside the big rock and fired three rounds quickly into the area before he rolled behind the ponderosa stump.

No return fire came.

Morgan looked around the far side of the stump, then ran low toward the target rock. Alonzo was there somewhere. The man had not carried a rifle when he dismounted. If he had one it had to be still on the Pinto.

Morgan crashed brush, letting Alonzo know he was coming. Then he stopped and listened. He could hear movement to the left going upstream. Alonzo or the third ambusher?

There was no way to know. Morgan ran hard through the brush, made it to the edge of the river and charged along the more open woods. He stopped behind a pine and listened. Again he heard someone running ahead of him, moving on upstream away from the horses, away from La Grande.

This direction headed into the Blue Mountains. Beyond them to the north and west lay Pendleton, about fifty miles away. Alonzo had no intentions of going that far. Where was he going?

Morgan ran ahead again making as little noise now as possible. The next two times he paused he heard the crashing ahead was closer. ALonzo was getting tired.

Morgan moved with no sound now working steadily forward. Every fifty feet he paused to listen. Then moved again. Closer and closer.

At a wide open spot Morgan saw Alonzo ahead. He turned and looked back. Morgan brought up the Spencer and slammed three shots at him. The last one caught Alonzo in the leg and he went down. He screamed something and crawled into the brush and out of sight.

Morgan moved more cautiously now, circling into the stream and across it so he could keep in the brushy area. He came out where he figured Alonzo had holed up. Good cover here allowed him to recross the stream in knee deep water.

He paused on shore and listened.

Nothing.

Morgan moved slowly toward where Alonzo must be. His leg could be broken from the shot. Good. After ten minutes of slow going, he came to a slightly more open place where the brush thinned out.

Movement. His eye caught something moving. Morgan concentrated on the spot and soon saw Alonzo's brown jacketed arm. Lee nodded and waited. That Sioux Indian had taught him patience during those training days. Once he and the Sioux had hidden behind a log and stayed there without moving for three hours.

Morgan watched the man's progress. He crawled, using his elbows and his feet. Morgan could have sent two .52 caliber lead slugs pounding into the gunman's head and ending it, but that wasn't good enough. Alonzo had to know. He had to realize he was dying. He had to pay back a little for all the pain he had caused.

Alonzo came to a place he could turn toward the river or go more inland. He turned toward the river and more cover. As he did his left leg showed plainly. Morgan lifted the Spencer and shot him in the upper thigh. But it was just a flesh wound. The damn weapon shot about two inches high.

The scream from Alonzo echoed down the beginnings of a canyon that led into a gorge.

"Bastard!" Alonzo screeched. "Damn bastard. That has to be you, Morgan. How did you know?"

"I knew, Alonzo. I knew you were a murdering bastard. You're a straight kill man. You're filth, you're shit. The world will be better off without you. I killed two of your bushwhackers. They were as dumb and stupid as you are."

Alonzo brought up his revolver and sent three

shots at Morgan's position, but the rounds fell short.

"You're gonna die, Alonzo. Your killing days are over. I can take you out anytime I want to. I want you to suffer a little more. Where do you want the next slug? In your arm or your belly?"

"You whore's whelp!" Alonzo screamed. "I'll kill you yet. Let's do a straight gunfight. I'm ready any time."

"Not a chance, killer. This isn't a sporting event. You tried to kill me with three hidden men. They all failed. Now it's your turn to taste more lead."

Alonzo was only half concealed. Morgan saw his arm and fired at it. He missed low and the slug tore through Alonzo's shirt but must have missed his flesh. In an instant Alonzo surged up to a crouch and darted into the heavy brush and behind a large tree. For the moment he was safe.

There was no sound for a minute. Morgan wanted to run forward, but Alonzo still had the six-gun and he was good with it.

A saddle creaked.

How did he get a horse? Morgan came up running. He surged into the brush toward the large tree. He panted as he got to it without drawing fire. Slowly Morgan inched around the tree. Thirty feet away he saw the back of a brown horse vanishing behind heavy brush and a stand of ponderosa.

Gone! No, just ahead there was a thirty yard wide open space. Morgan listened and was sure the horse moved that way. He sighted in on the open meadow where he figured Alonzo might come out.

Ten seconds later the big brown burst through the screen of brush into the open.

Morgan put the first shot through the horse's barrel chest. That slowed her. The second shot caught the mare in the side of the head and put her down.

Morgan had no hesitation at all about killing a horse. You kill the horse the man goes down, and then you can track the man. Simple. Uncomplicated.

The brown rolled. Alonzo tumbled free, seemed unhurt and ran upstream.

Again it was a cat and mouse game. This time it took Morgan more than a half hour to track down Alonzo. He was limping and trying to circle back to town.

Morgan's first shot caught Alonzo by surprise. He had just jumped a small stream and jogged into a meadow with no cover at all. The shot plowed up dirt in front of him and he stopped. Then he fell on his knees and let the revolver lower.

"Morgan, what do you want, damnit?"

"I want you to suffer some. How many men have you killed without giving them a chance? How many women? You're a killing son of a bitch who should die slowly, Alonzo."

Morgan shot him in the left arm.

Alonzo fell to the ground and screamed in pain. Morgan watched him in the grass, but a moment later he was gone, out of sight. Morgan stood to see better and Alonzo's six-gun barked twice. Morgan felt the round slice through his thigh but he bit off a scream of pain. He didn't want Alonzo to know he was hit. He dropped down and now saw the slight depression, a watercourse where Alonzo must be crawling downhill and out of sight.

Morgan ran parallel with the little gully, and when it emptied out at a small creek he was there waiting.

Alonzo looked behind him, grinned and stood. When he turned back he saw Morgan standing fifty feet in front of him with the Spencer leveled at his gut.

"Morning, Alonzo. Welcome to hell." Morgan shot him in the left leg breaking a bone, dumping Alonzo in the grass beside the stream.

The wounded man fired three times, but Morgan had ducked down even though he was out of range. He wanted no lucky shot to hit him.

"Bastard!" Alonzo screamed. He turned and crawled toward Morgan until he was in the open. Then he pushed and groaned and at last sat up.

"Now, Morgan, do it quick. Come into the open and make it a clean, quick headshot."

"This isn't like you, Alonzo. What are you playing here?"

Morgan saw the glint of the metal almost too late. He rolled to the left toward an old rotting log. A rifle snarled once, then twice, and again. The slugs ripped through the brush where Morgan had been. He lay perfectly still.

"I got him!" an excited voice said. "Told you we could do it if I waited."

"Yeah, waited. He almost killed me you stupid asshole! You got to make sure. Go over there and check."

"Not me. I tell you he's dead or damn near to it. I had him right in my sights. Them leaves was still moving when the first slug went in there."

"Leaves moving? You didn't *see* him when you shot?"

"Hell, he was right there. The blue smoke was

still coming up from his last shot."

By that time Morgan could lift his head and move a few leaves and see out to the opening where Alonzo sat. Alonzo was where he had been. He looked to his left, talking, evidently, to the third bushwhacker.

Morgan watched. The two kept arguing.

At last the bushwhacker gave in. He would check the corpse. But instead of doing it the safe way through the thick brush, he lifted out of the fringe of trees and stormed across the thirty yards of open space.

Morgan lifted his rifle and tracked the target's chest, led him a step and fired. The slug caught flesh and the side of the gunman's heart and dumped him into the little meadow dead with his face in the leaves.

"Now, Alonzo, it's your turn."

Morgan stood and walked out of the cover. Alonzo fired the last two shots in his six-gun, then frantically tried to reload.

"Won't help, Alonzo. It's time."

Morgan put one .52 caliber round through Alonzo Baer's forehead. The big slug jolted Alonzo's already dead body four feet backward and when the lead came out of the top of his head, it took a four inch divot of skull and brains with it.

Morgan let out a pent of breath he had held as he sighted in, then went to find the horses. He located his own and two others. He tied two bodies each on the two horses and led them back toward town. A quarter of a mile out of town he left them untied and rode back to the little shed where Charlie's horse had been stabled.

He unsaddled her, rubbed her down and gave

her a quart of oats. Then he went back to the newspaper office.

Both women looked at him as he came through the back door. Then both ran and hugged him.

"Thank god you're safe," Franny said.

"Mostly thanks to Morgan," Charlie said. "How many of them?"

"Four."

"All dead?"

"They'll be wandering into town soon as the horses get hungry."

"You're wounded!" Charlie said. "Your leg. Take your pants off."

Morgan hesitated.

"Lee, we both have seen you with your pants off. Now don't be silly. Drop your pants so we can work on your leg."

Charlie ran to get her doctoring kit and Franny crossed her arms under her breasts and watched him, a smile on her lips. He unbuckled his belt and let his pants down. The slug had tore through his left leg about mid thigh, but had cut only an inch of flesh and muscle. It hurt like crazy, but didn't interfere with his walking.

Franny pushed his short underwear up and stroked her hand through his genitals and grinned. "You're all soft and wormy," she whispered.

Charlie came back and looked at the two bloody spots. She wiped the blood off his leg and put some salve on the puncture wounds, applied a thick compress to help keep the bleeding from starting again, and then wrapped his leg with a bandage made from a sheet. When she was done she kissed the bandage and grinned.

"Mamma kissed it and made it well," she said.

Morgan pulled up his pants. "Thanks, I appreciate that. Now I won't bleed all over the banker's new floor. I have a date with Mr. Wert. He's gonna be surprised to see me."

"Don't get in any more trouble," Franny said. "Remember the Town Meeting is at one o'clock to hear Mr. Rutledge."

"Mostly he'll be listening, but at least it could make my front page story," Charlie said.

They watched him.

"Ladies, thank you again. I'll see you both at the Town Meeting."

He checked the loads in his Peacemaker Colt .45 and grim faced, walked out the front door.

When Morgan stepped in the bank the lackey at the desk stood up. Morgan motioned him to sit down. The man sat. Lee walked toward the President's door which he saw stood open a foot as if inviting him.

Morgan kicked it open and the banker jumped where he sat behind his desk. His hand darted to a drawer, but Morgan's big six-gun was out already and Wert's hand stopped.

"Both hands on the desk, slow and easy," Morgan said. He pushed the door closed and heard it latch.

"Now, you and I are going to have a small talk. Your four bushwhackers failed in their mission, I'm still alive. Right now you owe me one of two things. You ordered those men to kill me, which makes you just as guilty as they are. You should be joining them in a common grave. How does that sound?"

"No, I never did that. I don't know what you mean."

"You think Alonzo would come after me on his

own, with three riflemen? That's not even close, Wert."

The banker stood slowly, his hands nervous around his watch pocket.

"So you want your well deserved bullet in the head?"

"No! For god's sake, Morgan, let's be reasonable. I'm a businessman."

"And you have certain expenses. One of them was Alonzo Baer. He isn't working for you anymore. I want the five hundred you promised him to kill me. That's your second choice."

"I did no such . . ."

Morgan stepped forward and put the gun's muzzle against Wert's forehead.

"A bullet only costs three cents. I'll be glad to cover the cost of blowing your head off."

"No, wait. No! You have a point. I'll be glad to give you the money. Five hundred. Just put the gun away. You're safe here. I'll go get the money."

"Have the kid outside bring it," Morgan said.

Five minutes later Morgan walked out of the side door of the bank with the five hundred dollars in crisp new twenty dollar greenbacks.

He strolled down the street and saw the platform that had been built in the middle of the street. Red, white and blue banners decorated it. The Town Meeting was set for one o'clock and by the time on the clockmaker's display it was ten minutes to one.

Morgan pulled a chair out from the wall at the hardware store, sat down and tipped it until the back rested against the wall. He sat in the chair and closed his eyes, warming in the summer sun.

Chapter Fourteen

The meeting started right on time. Mason Rutledge spoke first.

"Good people of La Grande. This is my first visit here and I must say the natives are friendly. I've been to the Wallowas and to the Grande Ronde and across about half of your valley. I like this area. It's prime territory for development and expansion and I think the railroad will help that progress come before you know it.

"Now, enough of me. I came here to listen to you folks. I want to know what you think and where you would most like to have the railroad placed. Now I'm not saying this is a referendum. I can't promise to put the road in one place or another just because more people vote for one site. But the Great Western Railroad company wants to talk to you, and mostly listen to you. All right, Mr. Mayor. I'll turn the meeting back to you."

Slocum Wert was first on the list of speakers. He gave a stirring message about how the railroad through the Wallowas would mean doubling the size of La Grande in ten years and mean hundreds of extra jobs for residents.

It was about what they had heard in the meeting the other day. But he took it a step farther.

"Ladies and gentlemen, I can promise you that if we get regular rail transport to and from the Wallowas, that I will not only harvest the timber and replant the mountains, I will set up a resort on Wallowa Lake that will rival the best in the south or the east.

"I want something that will attract visitors here from all over the United States to take advantage of the beautiful scenery and the water of the magnificent lake."

There was a big cheer that went up.

"Of course, to do that I need to have rail transport to the Wallowas, and to the lake if possible. Thank you, Mr. Mayor."

To Morgan's surprise, Franny helped her grandfather up the steps to the platform and stood beside him as he presented the case for the town. He faltered halfway through and had to sit down quickly. Franny took over and finished the plea.

"I don't know all there is to know about this, like most of the rest of you. But the way I look at it is we take care of the town first, we bring the railroad through La Grande, and that will help it grow and then we can develop the outlying areas as we can afford to. Even Mr. Wert could still do this.

"My Grandfather and I strongly urge you, Mr.

Rutledge, to chose the shorter, better route through La Grande where 90 percent of the people in the county live and work, and which is the business and social hub for half of Eastern Oregon.''

When she was through two more men spoke for the La Grande route, then one for the Wallowas. Morgan walked up and asked the Mayor if he could speak.

"Open forum, young man. Anybody who wants to gets to talk here today.''

Morgan hooked his thumbs in his belt and stared out at the meeting. "Only been here a short time, but it doesn't seem like a hard choice to make. The railroad doesn't want to spend twice what it needs to put through a road. La Grande route is the best, but that doesn't mean the railroad can't serve Wert and his lumbering interests, as well.

"First, put the line in here, then run a spur line up to Catherine Creek to the mill. The railroad will then have the added economic advantage of both areas. All the business created here in town for freight and passengers, and the lumbering and even log business from the great stand of marketable timber in the Wallowas.

"Mr. Rutledge, I ask you to comment on this plan to include both with the use of a simple spur line.''

Rutledge stood beaming. "The gentlemen has hit the perfect solution. Going into the Wallowas the other way would have cost eighty percent more. But running a spur line across the valley land and into the mill site that I saw this morning, would be only a 15 percent increase in costs.

"Gentlemen, it will be my recommendation to

the board that we come through the Blue Mountains, down the Grande Ronde to La Grande and then on to Baker. We'll put the spur line in where it will serve Mr. Wert best for his lumber mill."

There was a shout, and then a general celebration. After about ten minutes the rejoicing eased and the people began to drift back to their homes and businesses. Then a bellow sounded from a side street.

Two little boys drove two horses ahead of them into Main Street.

A woman screamed and fainted in front of the Johnson Dry Goods Store.

A man swore and ran out and grabbed the reins of the two horses.

A deputy sheriff ran up and examined the four bodies that had been tied head down over the horses.

Sheriff Higgins walked over and looked at the men's faces. He called off names for three of the men.

"Don't know this other one. Probably a drifter." He looked around. "Anybody know what happened to this quartet? Alonzo Baer there is a gunman, everybody knows that. We also hear he's been working for Mr. Wert. Wert, what can you tell us? What do you know about this?"

Slocum Wert sniffed. "Sir, I know nothing about these four men. Mr. Baer has not been in my employ for over two weeks now."

Sheriff Higgins stared at him a minute. "There'll have to be a hearing. I'll want you there, and anyone else interested. Somebody killed these men, then made sure we know about it. I'll expect anyone with any facts about this situation to come forward and inform the sheriff's office."

Sheriff Higgins motioned to two men to lead the horses down to the undertakers. He stood there watching them walk away, then he began looking at the people at the meeting who hadn't drifted off.

Franny and Rudolph Merriweather walked up slowly to where Morgan stood leaning against a pole that held up the overhang in front of the Grande Ronde General Store.

"Well, whippersnapper," Merriweather said. "Looks like you saved the day for our little city with that compromise."

"Maybe. I'm sure the railroad had figured out the economics of it long before I said what I did. Rutledge's job was to come here and get the town and Wert to agree to some such deal. I just helped him out a little."

Morgan grinned. "Good to see you two getting along."

"Getting along? The hell you say. I'm damn near eighty-six years old. Oldest goat in town, which means I don't have to get along with any-body. The girl kid here is one of my managers. She's taking over my real estate division." He chuckled. "Come to think of it, that's the only division I have."

"You could always open up a fancy-lady house. Give Wert some real competition."

Merriweather fingered his chin in thought. "Yeah, now there is a great idea. Always have liked the ladies. I'd get used to the way they run around most naked after a bit. Course I'd have to interview and inspect each one . . . ."

"Grandpa, you wouldn't!" Franny said, her eyes flashing, her arms akimbo.

"Don't worry, the house will pay its rent on

time, and maybe a percentage." Rudolph Merri-weather was grinning now.

Franny let out a held in breath. "Thank god, you're teasing me."

They all laughed.

"Still sounds like a good idea," the old man said winking at Morgan.

Lee looked around. "Where's Charlie?"

"She said this was Wednesday again and she still hasn't got her lead story. I think this was it. I guess that I should go down there and help her."

Morgan looked at the old man. "You ever see a newspaper put together, old duffer?"

Merriweather laughed. "Not for a long time. Maybe I could shuffle along down there and watch."

"Watch," Morgan said. "The paper is just about at the break even point. I figure with the railroad it'll be a gold mine in three or four years. If you were to make an interest only loan to the paper for say five years, you'd be doing the town a real favor. Keeping a good editor/publisher in town and saving a fine little paper to serve the community."

"Mmmmmm. Might at that. If I get my whore-house. I'll take it up with my Real Estate Division Manager."

They all laughed and walked slowly down the two blocks to the La Grande *Observer* office. Charlie chewed on her pencil as she worked on the lead story. She looked up as they came in.

"Mr. Merriweather! I'm pleased you came down. What can I do for you?"

"Not the point, pretty young thing. Point is I might be able to do something for you. Just go on about your business. I'm here as an observer . . . and maybe I'll want to make a business loan to the editor/publisher."

Charlie scowled and stared at Morgan. He held up his hands and then grinned.

"Fine, Mr. Merriweather. I do have a lot to get done yet, this being Wednesday."

"I can find a chair and sit, not decrepit as some folks think."

Franny was grinning. She hadn't seen this side of her Grandfather in a long time.

"There. That will have to do for the lead story. Morgan, would you set it for me? Give you a big kiss if you do."

"Before or after?"

"After. I don't want to get you so excited you forget where the letters are in the type case."

Morgan took the two sheets of yellow paper and went to the back shop and the type case and began picking out the letters of the words, one by one, and putting them in the type holder. It was slow work.

It was mid-afternoon when Franny, who had been sitting and watching the front office, came back with a visitor.

"Kid Texas, hi," Morgan said.

The youth shook his head. "Mom says I can't call myself that any more. I'm Henry. What a dumb name."

Henry held his right arm in a white sling. The whole forearm and down to his fingers wrapped solidly in a plaster cast.

"Henry isn't such a bad name," Franny said. "We had a president named that, or was that Henry Clay?"

"What about Hank?" Morgan suggested. "That's a nickname lots of guys named Henry are called. Hank is a great name. What do you think?"

The youth brightened. "Yeah, I like that. I'll tell my mom that I'm gonna be Hank."

"Hey, Hank, you want to help me out around here? I'm getting more business now, and I could use some help. Can't pay much but it would be better than just laying around with a broken arm."

"Sure. What can I do?"

"My biggest problem is setting type. You know what type is? Have Morgan show you over there by the case. Best way to learn the case is by using it, and I bet you could pick it up real quick. Why don't you get a tablet off the front counter and draw out a picture of the case and write in where each of the small and capital letters go?"

"Yeah. Sounds interesting."

"Interesting," Morgan said. "It kept me from starving one winter." Morgan showed him the case. "I need to do the headline. The bigger type is up here. This is called a font. That's a bunch of individual letters like these all in one special kind of type."

By four that afternoon they had the front page set, locked in place and proof read. Charlie made two changes on words that were spelled wrong, then they locked it up again, pounded the type flat and put it on the press.

"Time out for food," Rudolph Merriweather said. "You're all my guests at Delmonico's. You too, Hank. Bet we can find something good to eat down there."

They had an early supper. The stew was good with lots of vegetables mixed in with the beef stew meat and rich sauce that doubled as gravy for the potatoes. They finished with pieces of pie. The vote was cherry pie, three; and lemon chiffon, two.

Mr. Merriweather excused himself. "I need to get back to my office and clean up a few business matters." He looked at Franny. "John Calder had a talk with you, didn't he? Everything worked out?"

"Yes, I'm going to take an office in the same building he's in next to the saddle shop. That's one of *our* buildings. I'll be starting first thing Monday morning. By then the office may be all done."

"Good. It's not too far away so I can drop in now and then." He looked at Charlie. "Charlene, you watch your nickels. If you need a few thousand here or there, you stop by and see my Real Estate manager. We can set up an interest only loan on an as you need it basis. If you need one."

Back at the newspaper office, Franny took a look at the books and made some suggestions about better bookkeeping. Charlie checked the sample and nodded.

"Set up the new system for me, and charge me for it. It'll help me save money in the long run."

Hank helped them until about six, then he said he had to go home. Charlie wrote a note to his mother explaining where he'd been all afternoon and asking if he could come and help her two days a week. He would get paid a quarter each day. She handed him a new shiny quarter and Hank yelped in delight.

They began printing off the paper.

"Six pages!" Morgan yelped. "That means I have to swing that damn heavy lever a thousand and eight hundred times?"

"The man's multiplication is amazing," Charlie said. She pushed another sheet of paper on the press and took it off as it printed.

"Look at it as an opportunity to serve La Grande," Franny said.

They worked steadily for an hour, then took a rest. Charlie brought coffee down and some chocolate cake she had made the day before.

Morgan sipped the coffee. "Hey, this morning when both of you.were prancing around upstairs bare to the waist, what were you trying to do? Surprise me, or what?"

"When we what?" Franny asked. "I certainly was not half naked this morning. You mean at breakfast?"

"Yeah. Both of you were bare halfway down, your tits just swinging and swaying."

"You must be having a spell again, Morgan. Fantasy world. You wished we were naked to the waist, so that's the way you saw us. Did we mention anything about it?"

"No. I thought that . . . "

"Did we act other than like we were normally dressed?"

"No, so I went along with you."

"And I suppose I went outside to get that note with my . . . my titties all bare and bouncing around?"

"No, when you came down to get the note you had on your blue work shirt."

"I wore that all morning, from the minute I got up."

"Hey, what are you two trying to do. This morning. . . ."

The both looked at him with frowns.

Morgan held up both hands. "I give up. I give up. I just imagined it. Now, let's get the rest of this paper printed before my arms fall off."

Chapter Fifteen

It was nearly ten that evening before they had the 300 papers all printed, collated and folded ready to be sent out to the stores and homes the next morning.

"I think a small drink upstairs would be in order," Charlie said.

"I should be getting back home," Franny said. "It's safe for me now, isn't it?"

"I'm sure you'll be fine," Morgan said. "Wert doesn't have any reason now to want to hurt you."

"Stay one more night here," Charlie urged. She smiled. "Maybe Lee will think we're running around half naked again. He has fantasies like that all the time."

Franny looked at Charlie and the girls smiled. They hurried up the steps to the apartment.

Charlie got a bottle of wine and Franny set out the glasses. When Morgan turned around he saw

Charlie come out of the bedroom, the blue work shirt she always wore when she printed was gone and she was bare to the waist.

"You're doing it again," Morgan said.

"What?"

"Charlie, not that I mind, but you're half naked."

Charlie groaned and shook her head. "I just don't know what we're going to do with you, Lee Morgan. You better not spread these kinds of wild stories around. Franny, what are we going to do with Morgan? He thinks I'm half naked again."

He turned and saw Franny standing by the table pouring wine. She too, now was bare to the waist.

"Morgan, you must control your sexual fantasies," Franny said. "We talked about that this afternoon."

Morgan grabbed Franny's hand and then caught Charlie's. He pulled them with him into the bedroom and gently pushed them down on the bed. Then he sat between them and began fondling their breasts, one with each hand.

He didn't say a word. He bent and kissed them alternately and then moved to kiss their breasts.

At last Franny yelped, "Oh, god, I can't stand it anymore!" She sat up and grabbed Morgan and kissed him. She pushed him down and rolled on top of him, her hips humping at him a dozen times.

Charlie sat up and grinned. "We had you going again, didn't we? You thought you must have imagined the whole thing this morning. How could you tell. We stuck to our stories."

Morgan let up on Franny a moment and kissed

Charlie, and then sucked one of her breasts into his mouth as she sighed.

When he came up for air he lay between the women as they quickly kicked out of their skirts and hose and began to undress him.

"Admit it, Morgan. You really didn't know what to think this morning, did you?" Franny asked. "Then when we denied being topless, you began to wonder if you had imagined it."

"Not a chance. I knew you two were mad because I had been making love to both of you. Just a crazy woman way of getting back at me. I knew it all the time."

"Did not!" Charlie said.

"Did too!"

They all laughed.

"At least now we know for sure who is what and when is how and that we're going to have a wonderful time before morning." Morgan said, "First, let me go bring in that wine. No sense in wasting it now that it's been opened and halfway poured."

He brought back the wine and they sat on the bed all naked and grinning at each other, fondling, touching, exploring. The wine glasses emptied and then emptied again.

"You know you have to do us both at once," Charlie said softly.

"Both at once?" Morgan asked.

"Yes, silly," Franny said. "One with your prick and the other one with your mouth."

"Sounds fair."

"Show me," Charlie said and stretched out on the bed. Morgan looked at her a minute then lay Franny down the opposite way beside her. He slid into Charlie easily and moved Franny up farther until her waist was about right. Then he leaned over and spread her legs and began lapping up her juices.

"My god, I think he's got it," Franny said. By then all three were so worked up nobody could laugh as they all went charging along to sexual fulfillment.

Franny exploded first, humping and shaking and moaning loud and long. Charlie powered into her climax with a shattering series of spasms that left her shaken and drained. Morgan jolted into her hard eight times, his own body spasming in the ancient seed planting thrust.

Ten minutes later they had revived and sat side by side on the edge of the bed. Each had a glass of wine.

"I think this is going to be a nice party," Franny said. She wasn't used to this much wine this fast.

Charlie stared bleary eyed at them. "It's already a great party," she said.

"Gonna be a real wild party. We need Ming here, too," Morgan said.

Franny shook her finger at him. "Not true, not true, not true. We're the three cavaliers! We're friends and lovers forever!'"

They had to drink to that.

By midnight all three of them were in various stages of being drunk. Franny had passed out on one side of the bed. Charlie insisted on one more loving, but the booze and the four times already had left Morgan less than a sturdy lover. He gave up after two more tries.

"How long since you slept three in a bed?" Charlie asked.

She didn't wait for an answer, just grinned and

passed out.

Morgan moved her to the other side of big bed and claimed the middle for himself. Halfway through the night he realized that meant he was getting kicked and pushed from both sides.

Morgan woke up first with daylight. He leaned up on his elbows and watched one girl, then the other. Franny so honey blonde and Charlie so dark headed. Both slept soundly. He eased from the bed and dressed and moved to the kitchen.

He got the fire going quietly, then boiled coffee, found fixings and mixed up hot cakes and fried the bacon. When he was ready, he went into the bedroom and kissed them both awake.

"Morning," he said.

"Go away, far away!" Franny said.

"Can't be morning, not already!" Charlie mumbled.

Slowly they sat up, looked at each other and grinned.

"Breakfast will be ready in five minutes, ladies. Hotcakes, coffee, bacon and eggs. Hurry, hurry."

Morgan grinned as he watched them jump up naked and begin to hunt for clothes. They quickly pushed him out the bedroom door and closed it.

Someone brought a message to the newspaper office that Mr. Merriweather wanted to see Morgan before noon. He took his time shaving and put on a clean shirt, then walked into the Gunsmoke Saloon just after eleven.

Ormley stared at him with no pleasure.

"You've become the damn fair haired boy around here," Ormley said.

"Practice. Ormley, you practice enough and you'll make it to the big money some day, too."

Morgan walked past the bar and back to Merriweather's private office. He knocked once and went in.

Merriweather sat there sipping on a cold bottle of beer. He put it down and grinned.

"Doc Stanton says a man my age can stand a shot of beer now and then to clean out the system. After he told me that, I paid my bill." He laughed and then wheezed.

"By damn, I feel ten years younger. You been good for me, boy. Done shook up Fran too, I see. She'll do good with the property. I know that. We'll go see the judge this fall and get that competency thing settled and to top it all, the damn railroad is coming!"

"Still want me to earn that thousand dollars?" Morgan asked with a grin. "I can do it."

"Oh, no doubt. I saw those four you brought in on horseback yesterday. Mighty nice job. One of them with a knife. Them were the four who tried to bushwhack you, I'd wager."

He looked up at Morgan but Lee remained silent.

"Yeah, I like a man who knows when to keep his yap shut. Remember the first day you came in here?"

"Like it was two weeks ago."

Merriweather slapped his knee and laughed. He wheezed so he took a shot of the cold beer.

Then he reached in his desk drawer and took out a stack of bills. He spread them out on his clean desk.

"Wanted to tell you that you earned that thousand, *by not killing me*. Hell, I got more than

I wanted now. Got the railroad, got my grand-daughter working with me. And by damn! I'm still alive."

He pawed the bills together and handed them toward Morgan.

"Go on, take it. You more than earned it. Nobody else in town gonna give you anything."

Morgan took the bills, folded them and pushed them in his shirt pocket and fastened the button.

"If I offered you a good job, would you stay, Morgan?"

"Nope."

"Didn't reckon you would. You're not an eight to five kind of man. How about if I arranged for you to marry Franny. Have a good woman and all of my money, after a while. Would you go for a package like that?"

"Nope."

"Didn't reckon you'd like that one either."

He fished a cold bottle of beer from an iced bucket in back of the desk, opened it and passed it to Morgan.

"Hear you're from over in Idaho."

"Out of Boise aways."

"The Spade Bit. Your dad came through here now and again. Met him once. He was quite a man, that father of yours."

"True."

"You headed that way?"

"Probably."

They sat there drinking the beer, not saying a word. When the beer was gone, Morgan stood.

"Been a damn fine couple of weeks, Lee Morgan. Glad you stopped by." He held out his hand.

"Glad I came by myself," Morgan said. He took

the hand and shook it, then met the old man's gaze and returned it. A man's look, an equal, a friend.

Morgan turned and walked out the door. He didn't even speak to the barman or Ormley.

He was itching again. The old itch that got him moving down the trail. No time for one more go round with the ladies. No last romp in the bedroom or on the floor.

It had been a pair of weeks.

He went to the livery and paid for the keep of his horse. Then gave her to the stable boy.

"She's not much use, but she's yours if you want her. I got no paper. Get some and I'll write you a bill of sale for a dollar."

"Don't got no dollar," the stable boy said, his face going from unbelieving joy to despair.

"Don't need a dollar," Morgan said. "That just makes it legal." He wrote out the bill of sale, signed it, got the livery man to witness it and went down to see when the stage east left town. Two o'clock.

A few minutes later, Charlie looked at him with a combination of sadness and memories.

"We had a good time, Morgan," she said. "I'll never forget you. Never."

"Forget me soon, button, and get yourself married. Enough of these wild sex parties. And if you run a little short of cash, you have that letter of credit with the Merriweathers."

She kissed him and hugged him so tight he was afraid he'd lose his breakfast.

"Oh, damn, I wish you'd stay."

"Ain't the staying kind."

"You're darned right you ain't. I knew that the first time I saw you come in the front door."

"You let me stay anyway."

"Yeah. Once in a lifetime a woman gets a chance at a man like you, so I took my chance. No regrets."

He kissed her mouth gently, then touched the tip of her nose and walked out the door without looking back. He marched down to Delmonico's for a big steak. It was gonna be one hell of a long stage coach ride to Boise.